HE WAS MURDERED

BOOK ONE OF MURDER TRILOGY

PRASAD BABU GALLA

To Lover of Books

To my favorite Authors Agatha Christie, Ajay K. Pandey,
and Novoneel Chakraborthy.

To my favorite Indian filmmaker Ram Gopal Varma (RGV),
who inspires me daily with his crime movies.

To my parents Galla Demudu and Galla Rama Lakshmi,
who gave me birth to this stupid creative genius, my
brother Galla Bharat who tolerated me since my
childhood, my wife Galla Prabandha who had to bear me
lifelong, and my little panda Galla Himansh for being my
son.

Contents

Contents

Preface

I had written this because it was so difficult to do that the idea had fascinated me. The man who was murdered was related to an aspiring author who was in search of a true story for his debut crime novel. Destiny planned in another way as he was the suspect in the murder case. This is the story of an author, how he came out of the

Prologue

July 2017

It was a rainy day with kisses of raindrops flowing about him. He lost his way in the dark dense forest. Someone was walking before him holding a sharp-edged vegetable cutting knife, the blood flowing like drops of an ocean from that edged knife and he had been for quite some time hiding behind the tree.

His eyes were used to blur due to the rain in the darkness and moved on the wet leaves which made a bit sound. The person turned back and had not seen his face, was running from and some moment he stopped. And he looked back, but still, the person was chasing him. So, he ran and paused for a moment to catch his breath.

Prasad started running again. He checked the message he received: *You can't run from your karma.* He couldn't shout for help because there was nobody in the forest. He noticed a light in the distance which gave him hope. He took a breath and ran towards it, approached the light, he saw an abandoned wooden house. He peeped in through the window and his breath regained a normal pace. There were full of mirrors on four walls of the room with two lanterns placed on two corners of the room. He lost the image of his reflection in the mirror. It's invisible in every mirror, slowly an image occurred in front of him but it's not his image. The face of the image looks grunted, half damaged face with no eyes, a small nose, and two snake heads dancing out of his mouth. After some moment, his own image came out between the two snake heads from his mouth in the mirror.

'Hello, Prasad!' the Prasad inside the mouth in the mirror said to the one outside. The two snakes came out of the mouth in the mirror rolled his body and the Prasad inside the mouth said aloud,' *Your Karma is on the way, Babu.'* The two snakes hugged him very tightly at a time. He started to lose her senses and he can't raise his hands as they were tightened by the snakes. There was nobody to help him and suddenly the door was pushed by the person who chased him. Then the two snakes left him and the image in the mirror had disappeared, and back to normal. His own image was visible in all mirrors. But the person who chased him in the forest holding the bloodstained knife, standing in front of him. The person removed a sack from his covered face slowly and it was his own image standing before him. He was helpless and wanted to escape. He ran and found a door behind his back, tried to open it but he couldn't open it. He banged hard, kicked it a few times and he was falling from his own bed.

He opened his eyes wide. All he could see was his rotating ceiling fan. For a moment Prasad thought he was still in his nightmare. He relaxed and looked at his phone, it was morning around five forty-five. He had visited the contacts list on his mobile and searched the name Akbar and phoned him.

'Good morning, Today I want to propose Fathima.'

'Good morning, dude, at last, you took a good decision, but first, we have to warn him,' Akbar said in a sleepy voice.

'This evening we will meet him. Tell Aditya to arrange a meeting with him.' Prasad ended his call and fetched some water.

He moved to his bathroom, brushed his teeth, and showered naked by remembering her name, smiling by seeing his face in the mirror. Then he remembered the nightmare he had this morning and smiled back, how disgusting a dream it was, said to himself and moved out of the bathroom.

'Prasad!! Come, have a breakfast.' His dad called him from downstairs.

'Yes! Dad, coming.' Prasad said, wearing a white tee and blue jeans, moved down the steps and reached to the downstairs.

They both had breakfast, idly and spicy tomato chutney, which was made by his dad.

He moved quickly out of his home in a hurry, took his new black Royal Enfield Classic 500 Stealth, and reached Akbar's home, sounding horn.

Akbar came out of his home and started moving on the same bike. They both moved to the Alpha Restaurant near Akbar's home and ordered the spicy chicken fry Biriyani with a starter of chilly prawns. They chilled some time there and moved.

'I had the same disgusting nightmare yesterday, which came about a week ago on the same day.' Prasad said, looking at his phone.

'You mean, you were dreaming the same on every Saturday.' Akbar responded.

'Yes, someone was murdered in the forest which was witnessed by me. The murderer chased me, I ran and found an abandoned home with mirrors, but no image reflection except on one mirror, with no eyes, a small nose....

Two snake heads from a mouth, your own image between two snakes, rolled you and the man who chased you was your own image. Akbar interrupted his conversation and continued,' I was listening to the same story since our first year, now we were in the last year of our college.'

'Okay, let's move to college now.' He took bike keys from his pocket and left.

They reached college around evening four for their Electrical and Electronics Department special farewell party. That evening Aditya arranged a meeting with Mohan Krishna at their college canteen.

'Hey, how dare you get closer to my girlfriend,' Prasad shouted at him.

'From today, you shouldn't talk or be around her,' Akbar warned him.

'She is our Babu's girlfriend, be far from her, otherwise you don't know what will happen to you further,' Aditya advised him.

The three monkeys warned MK one by one, but he was watching them like a gentleman in a theatre without any expressions.

'I can't understand whom you are talking about.' Mohan Krishna said in innocence.

'Don't act smart buddy, we were talking about Fathima,' Aditya mumbled.

'Is she Babu's girlfriend? Does she know that? ' Mohan questioned Aditya.

'Babu will propose to her today, so you better keep away from her,' Akbar explained.

Mohan Krishna chuckled loudly and declared, 'We have been in love with each other since our 1st year.'

They knew that they love each other, but acted like they don't know at all.

'Whatever happened till now, leave it, she is mine now... She......is......mine.......now.' Prasad warned him.

Mohan Krishna knocked a shot on Prasad cheeks, it became pale rosy. His friends watched them like a movie without executing any battles. They dragged Prasad back to save his life from him.

'Your death is in my hands. Save your life from me. I don't know when I will kill you.' Prasad alerted him even he got knocked a shot from MK.

They left the place and moved into 'Durga Bar and Restaurant.' They ordered three large Kingfisher Strong Beers and a Spicy Onion Chips packet.

They completed the first round, then the second, and finally the third round.

'Will...... you kill...... him really?' Inquired Aditya.

'Hush.... don't reveal...... outside. I will pl....an and kill that bloody lover. Does he snatch Fathima away from me?' Prasad said in an intoxicant bang.

Where's this beard and weird man, Ak......bar? Prasad asked Aditya.

Aditya pointed his finger behind the table, he was already sleeping under the table intoxicated and they both too followed him.

1

5 YEARS LATER

March 2022

He was walking alone in the night to the car parking from downstairs of his office. He heard some strange voice around him. He moved fast with fear, heard some footsteps, and increased his pace of walking. He felt someone was pulling him behind, turned back, but no one was there. He walked very quickly and the decibels of strange sounds increased. He ran and ran looking back, he found someone was chasing him. He reached at his car, taking the car keys from his pocket, but his hands were twisted back. He was ready to shout for some help, but his voice was muted unexpectedly. He moved now with the heavy pace of walking out of the apartment to reach the road.

His eyes were used to the darkness by now. He kept running, unsure of his direction. He was still unable to find the road, he was trapped only in the same car parking area.

He saw a face-covered person in the middle of the car parking area, wearing a black suit holding a vegetable cutting knife, murdering the other person.

The murderer saw him, ran towards him, stabbed into his stomach, and slowly uncovered his face. It was Prasad.

He shouted after seeing his image.

He opened his eyes wide. All he could see was a static ceiling fan. He saw Prabha lying by his side, her face turned away from him. For a moment Prasad thought he was still in his nightmare. He forcibly turned Prabha's face towards him, hugged and relaxed. It was the month of March and Visakhapatnam was at an average high temperature and relative humidity. He had a habit of using a heavy blanket to cover himself in any season. He had seen the same dream one more time and that too only on Saturdays.

'What happened?' Prabha asked in a sleepy voice.

'Nothing, go back to sleep,' Prasad said.

Prabha closed her eyes.

He picked up his Samsung Galaxy S4 phone from beside his pillow, it was around 4:45 in the morning. He was about to get up to fetch some water on an empty stomach. He moved to jog at Railway Park near his home.

'Hello Mr. Writer, when will you publish your debut novel?' One of the joggers named Anand asked him embarrassingly.

'It will be soon, Uncle Ji,' he said in frustration.

And he walked out from there and the Kirana Shop owner chuckled and asked him,' Babu Ji, Will you publish your debut novel this year or after my granddaughter's marriage?'

'Everyone wants the next-door life; they don't know what's going on in their house.' he mumbled and fake smiled.

He reached home after jogging and drank a full bottle of water. He removed his sweat tee and asked for special coffee from his lovely sweetie, sometimes he calls her sweetie. He changes her name according to the situation's demands.

His beautiful innocent wife walked like a Barbie doll towards him, holding a cup of special coffee with one hand and the newspaper in another hand.

'Hey beauty, today you look very luscious and awesome.' whispered by kissing her long hair. She sighed and handed him a special coffee.

They both settled on a giant sofa placed on a balcony disseminating a special coffee in the beautiful dawn with a view of fascinating cliffs around his building.

They showered, had breakfast, and chit-chatted for some time.

Prabha removed her favorite red and blue combination saree from the wardrobe to wear for the luncheon invitation by Akbar. She also took a perfect match of a red tee and blue jeans for Prasad.

He was receiving continuous calls from Akbar to come before, not exactly to lunch.

She was still not ready yet, Prasad forcing her to ready quickly as he was getting pressure from Akbar.

Finally, she came out of the room, wearing a beautiful saree with traditional jewelry on her neck. He praised her beauty, but she interrupted him and said,' It's not a time to praise my beauty. Akbar was waiting there.'

He smiled and took his bike key, moving from their house.

2

They reached Akbar's home around morning eleven on his bike. They were so excited as his friend Akbar invited him to his home after a long time that too with his life partner. After Prasad's marriage, this was the first time they both were going to someone's home for a Biryani luncheon Party.

During his first year of engineering, Akbar invited him to the party, but after that, he became stingy, but still, he was always his bestie.

They were climbing the stairs to Akbar's floor. It was about 12:30 in the afternoon when he knocked on his door. His mom opened it and welcomed them in.

As Prasad had often been there, she knew him very well, but the first time he was with his beautiful partner. For him, Akbar's home never meant too many formalities. He was with his partner, so he acted politely and maturely. He had some water when Akbar's mother told him that he was not at home and his mobile was switched off.

'Wow! And he asked me not too late.' Prasad murmured.

A little later, there was another knock on the door. As Akbar's mom was in the kitchen, Prasad got up from his couch to open it. It wasn't Akbar, it was Akbar's dad.

'How are you, Prasad? How are you, Prabha?' Akbar's dad said politely to them.

'How much polite was Akbar's dad, my dad was also there, he was never polite with me.' He thought himself comparing fathers.

'We were fine, uncle. How are you?' Prasad and Prabha responded.

'I am fine, He's not on time all the time to home.' he said irritated.

For the next half an hour, the three of them talked, while they both ate lunch made by Akbar's mother without Akbar. This might not sound decent, but nobody could predict his arrival.

'The Biryani was very tasty and spicy, aunty.' Prasad said to Akbar's mom.

'Thank you, Babu.'

After lunch, they both moved to the giant couch in the living room, sitting comfortably.

'How about publishing your first book?' Akbar's dad asked Prasad.

'Uncle, I was searching for a real story to launch the debut of my first novel.'

'I don't know how much time it takes to get it published.' Prasad mumbled.

Prasad called Akbar from his mobile, but his mobile was still switched off.

It was around 4 p.m., and everyone was waiting for Akbar.

A little later, there was another knock. Akbar's mom opened the door.

'What happened to your mobile? Why do you keep it switched off?' Akbar's mom shouted, opening a door.

'No Charging, mom,' Akbar sang aloud.

Prasad managed his anger toward him and acted very polite as he was around his wife and Akbar's parents. He observed Akbar's face and he was feeling tense. He asked the reason for getting late and he said, simple sorry to both of them. Prasad has never seen him before. He was worried about something.

'He was hiding something.' Prasad thought to himself. Prasad said bye to him but there was no response from him. They both said bye to aunty and uncle and left there with some kind of unhappiness in their hearts. They left his home around evening four.

While driving to his home, Prasad received a phone call from an unknown number. He ignored that call as he was on driving. But still receiving repeated calls from the same number. So, he stopped his bike aside and answered the call.

'Hey dude, how are you? Have you forgotten me? It's Suresh, Suresh Kumar Sahoo.' he communicated on a phone.

'I am fine, man. What's happening? No calls, No Texts, you changed your contact. We were trying to reach you.'

'Cool man, I came to Visakhapatnam, waiting for you at beach road. Come alone, Let's meet here.'

'Alone! Why man.'

'I want to go quickly. If they come, they were not let me go back.'

'Ok man, I will be within an hour.'

Prasad dropped her wife at home and reached beach road around evening 5:15. He was very excited to meet him after a long time searching around for him but he was nowhere. He dialed his number but the mobile has been switched off. He sat on the green bench watching at the seashore.

It's almost half an hour waiting for him and dialed his contact again but it's still switched off. He bought a water bottle, washed his dusty face and took a handkerchief from his pocket, rubbed his wet face with plaina brown colored handkerchief. He sat again on the same green bench. Some bald man asked him for a pen as he was writing a love letter to propose to his girlfriend. Prasad was some frustrated and angered by his friend Suresh but still, he fakes smiled and was given his new blue point pen.

He received a call but not from Suresh, it was Aditya. He walked a few steps away as he can't hear the voice due to the noise around him. He doesn't want to tell him that he had been fooled by someone in the name of Suresh. He ignored his calls as if he knows Prasad was at beach road, he will force him to come to his home as his home was near beach road just 15 minutes to reach.

Prasad looked back and he have not found that bald man. No matter about the bald man but he was searching for him as he took his new blue point pen. He tried calling Suresh once again but his phone was still switched off. So, he moved from there and reached straight to his home around 7:30 p.m.

He showered and dressed, took the couch to sit comfortably, and thought about the call he received.

On that night around eight, someone knocked the door. Prasad got up from his giant couch to open it as his wife was in the kitchen cooking for dinner. He pulled it open to shouts of, 'Oh.... Dude.... Come in!'

It was Akbar. 'Hi Babu,' he greeted Prasad with a fake smile. Seeing his face, Prasad realized that he was still not right. He also greeted, smiled, and welcomed him in. He thought to not ask the reason for behaving strangely this afternoon. He decided to make him happy tonight and they recalled their college days. His partner called for dinner and they had dinner together.

Prasad was still confused about Akbar's behavior on that afternoon and why now he came again. But still, he managed to laugh and he was also making some jokes. They both were laughing again and again.

Prasad wants to talk about the strange call he received but again he thought not to tell him now. They both moved to Prasad's room and had an amazing time. Talking about their past and present. About those minimum girls in their class. About lecturers, his broken love, his friends, and his enemies. About ragging and many other good and bad things in their college days.

They talked about their jobs. They both kept talking for hours that night. It was around night eleven., Akbar looked sleepy, smiled, and looked at Prasad. He understood that it was Akbar's sleeping time and he had to leave now.

While Akbar leaving the place, he smiled again and whispered around Prasad's ears,' I talked about your nightmare with my uncle, psychiatrist Mr. Chowdhury. We have to go this Wednesday night at eight.'

'Thanks, buddy.' He said in a very low tone.

Akbar left Prasad's place with a grand smile on his face by saying good night to both Prasad and Prabha.

On the next day morning, Prasad relaxed on his couch, and switched on a fan, after completing his morning jogging. He picked up a water bottle and drank, removing his sweat tee.

Prabha gave him the special coffee, holding a newspaper in another hand. She settled beside him on the couch comfortably.

He gazed first at the movie page of the newspaper, read all the headlines from the front page, and stuck at the below of the front page titled 'He Was Murdered'.

He was murdered

Date: 21/05/2022

VISAKHAPATNAM: A man named MK alias Mohan Krishna was murdered at RK Beach Road in Visakhapatnam of Andhra Pradesh on Sunday evening. Police have formed two special teams to nab the culprit.

The 27-year-old was working as a software engineer in a Wipro company at Waltair of Vizag. He was going to marry Fathima next week, but He was found with injuries on his neck. He was lying on the ground and was battling for life. Immediately, some people rushed him to King George hospital where doctors declared him dead.

Police officials said that a deep injury was found on the neck of the boy. He had two minor injuries on his hands. Police suspected that minor injuries might have been self-inflicted ones. The police found a knife used for cutting vegetables. He was murdered with that. The police seized the knife.

G. Raghav Sai, Sub-inspector of Police, Visakha district, said that two special teams had been formed to probe the murder of Mohan Krishna.

He had an intense feeling as he finished reading the article. Even though the murdered one was his enemy in his college, He slipped a special coffee from his hands made for him by his beautiful wife. He took his mobile to call his friends but suddenly his phone vibrated as he kept on silent when going jogging this morning.

'Oh my gosh, I received 22 missed calls and one message from Akbar and Aditya,' he murmured himself.

He read a text message from Akbar, 'Let's meet at our favorite spot today evening at 6 p.m.'

The same text was forwarded to him by Aditya also.

'Content was ready. Now it's time to publish your first novel.' His wife declared, reading the same article.

'Where's the content? What were you talking about?' Prasad questioned her.

'Hush, He was murdered, the story of Mohan Krishna.' his wife announced the title of his debut novel.

He was motivated by his wife but he was thinking about who murdered MK.

That evening around 6:30 p.m., he reached their favorite spot on his bike. *The two monkeys were already waiting for me on the green bench and the third monkey is going to join them, he thought.* It's their favorite place, Thenetti Park, with a calm and magnificent view of the seaside. They used to bunk college and lingered here for the ranking of beauties.

'Welcome my dear murderer, you took five years to murder him,' Aditya alleged.

'Well planned and finally killed him, I never expected my best friend was a murderer,' Akbar confirmed.

'Cool buddies, I was not a murderer. I don't have any involvement in his murder.' Prasad clarified.

'Then you told us you will kill him that day,' they both said at a time.

'I was not a criminal or murderer to kill human beings. That day, I said everything in anger, frustration, and hangover. I don't have any intention to kill him. I have forgotten this matter on that day only.' He explained them clearly.

The three minds thinking about the murderer. Then suddenly Prasad received a call from his wife and lifted her call.

'Baby (sometimes his wife calls him), you better go to the police station and meet police Raghav for the story. You may get the details of the murder.' his wife said in a low sweet tone.

'Ok baby......Muah...Muah...bye see you.' kissed her on the phone and ended the call.

'So, guys, now we were going to meet the police Raghav,' he declared like a political party leader.

'Think once again, I heard Raghav was a dangerous person,' Aditya warned them.

'No problem, dudes, I will manage na,' Akbar said.

4

I never stepped into the police station in my life, Prasad thought to himself. He took his bike and ride to the police station to meet the police on the same night at around 7 p.m. They informed the head constable Mr. Venkatesh to meet Mr. Raghav. He told them to wait for one hour as Raghav was not available.

Raghav arrived at the police station around 8:45 p.m. and enquired about them with his constables. He called them inside his office room. They moved inside the office and stood in front of him.

'Hello guys, tell me how can I help you?' Raghav asked.

They were shivering and unable to talk, as they have seen the fire of the policemen on crime news channels and in movies. They also heard about the strictness and sincerity of Raghav.

Prasad opened his mouth with some fear on his body and talked, 'Sir we want to discuss the murder of Mohan Krishna.'

Then one after one, the other two also started talking without any fear.

'Hey, you wait. I am there na. I will ask him.' Akbar interrupted him and continued.

'Sir, have you found the murderer of MK? Still, how much time do you need? Close this case as soon as possible.

We need to know the murderer. We can't wait......We heard that you can solve any case within twenty-four hours. But why is this case still not solved?' questioned and warned the strict police officer.

Aditya and Prasad were observed the face of the police, his face looked tomato red. They understood what will happen next to them. They both grabbed Akbar but he was not controlling his words.

The policeman fake smiled, hiding his angriness but it burst out.

'Hey Venkatesh, I thought only one murderer was involved in the MK case, but now one murderer and two supporters.' The police laughed and informed the constable pointing his finger at them one by one.

They were watching their faces in confusion mode. They were clarifying at a time to him why they came to the police station.

'Shut up guys. Keep Silence. Now tell me who you are? What's the connection between the dead man and the three of you? Why were you here?' the police interrogated.

'Ok sir, I will tell you in full detail,' Prasad said.

'No, no, I will tell you, sir.' Akbar interrupted.

'Not you both, I will tell him,' Aditya mumbled.

'Hey stop you, idiots, tell one by one.' the police shouted at them.

'Sir, my name is Prasad Babu Galla, the writer,' Prasad told.

'To which movie?'

'Sir, not for movies, I write books.'

'Oh great, Venkatesh! Bring a cool drink to the writer sir.'

'Sir, tell him to bring milk for me,' Aditya asked innocently.

The policemen looked angry at him, and Aditya turned his face down.

And the police again questioned Prasad, 'How many books have you written up to now?'

'Still not counted.'

'Sir, how can he count? My hero wrote Zero.' Aditya interrupted and laughed. The police pointed his middle finger at him. Aditya shut his mouth.

'Venkatesh, drink cancel.' the police shouted.

'Sir, what about milk?' Aditya asked.

'Do you need milk? Take this, the police took his baton and beat two on his legs. Aditya shouted and shut his mouth permanently.

'You are a writer,' pointing his finger at Prasad.

'Then what about you both? 'Asked them in anger.

'I am Aditya, an Electrical Engineer in a private company,' Aditya replied.

'You shouted at me before. Why are you silent now?' the police asked Akbar.

'Sorry sir, I am Akbar, a cement business dealer,' Akbar replied.

The policeman Raghav's mobile was ringing, he picked up his Apple iPhone mobile from the table. He lifted the call and said them pointing his finger, 'Ok guys, you can leave now. Whenever I call you for interrogation, you have to cooperate with us. Now you three were our suspects.' the police informed us.

'Venkatesh, note down their names, address, and their contact numbers,' Raghav ordered his constable and continued his call.

They had given their information details and left the police station.

5

They left the police station and moved to their favorite place, beach road in Visakhapatnam. They sat on the green bench located on the seashore of the beach. They bought and ate the spicy moori mixture, thinking about the murder case.

'Hey, you should call Prabha and inform her the matter happened in the police station as she was the reason to meet the police,' Aditya said looking at Prasad's face.

Prasad took his mobile from his pocket, having already eight missed calls from his wife.

'I don't know why my sweet heart keeps worrying even though I'm at her nearby itself,' Prasad said, dialing her wife.

'Hello, dear, what happened?' He called her wife back.

'Baby, where are you? Come home. Now!' His wife sounded petrified.

Prasad's heart skipped a beat. Something terrible must have happened.

'What's wrong, my dear?' Prasad sounded equally terrified.

There was no response for a moment and then her wife said calmly, 'Nothing. I'm just feeling lonely. Come home now, Baby!'

This was strange. Suddenly her wife sounded as if everything was alright. 'You scared me, my sweetheart. Anyway, I'm coming home. Just we left the police station.'

'Come fast. We have to go out for dinner to your dad's place.'

'Today?'

'Yes, Today. In a few hours. So come home immediately.'

'Okay, dear. I'm coming.'

'What happened?' Aditya and Akbar asked him.

'Nothing. I need to go now. Have a luncheon to attend, Prasad said, taking his bike keys from his pocket.

'With Bhabhi?' Aditya gazed at him.

Prasad shot him a glance and said,' Yes but to my dad's place.'

Aditya and Akbar were muted and said,' After five years, he invited you?'

'Yes, I don't know, why now.' Prasad shrugged.

'Your father wants to transfer his all assets to your name.' Akbar sounded.

Prasad rolled his eyes' realizing Akbar was right. How could he have missed that? But I think it's not the time to transfer.

'Wish me luck,' Prasad said and left.

A few hours later, Prasad reached his home, and his wife waiting in the living room. He showered and wore the black suit, which was gifted by his father. Even though they have not talked in the past five years, his father gifted him, the black suit on his last birthday. His wife was surprised after seeing him in the black suit as he rejected this gift when his dad gifted him. She was happy to see him wearing the suit and a smile on his red cheeks. They drove in his Alto from Gajuwaka to Madhurawada. He would not take his bike for long drives. Prasad was more nervous as he became a suspect in the murder case and also more excited at an unexpected invitation from his father. His tears rolled down until his wife controlled him. He smiled and pretended.

They reached in a few hours and were received warmly by his father on their arrival.

'So nice to see you, my son,' he said, hugging Prasad. Prasad thought it was a long time to hug his father, it was odd that every father and son were fighting for nothing.

'It's been a while since I met you, dad,' Prasad added.

Five years, may not be that much longer, but it's very long for me, dad. Prasad thought to himself. They settled on a spacious L-Shaped couch. It was posh and neatly kept.

One woman entered with pulpy orange drinks from the kitchen room and kept them on the table located before the couch. Prasad and his wife stared at her unknowingly. They have never seen her before, she was wearing an expensive saree including jewelry on her broad neck.

They took pulpy drinks and sipped, waiting for the women's introduction from Mr. Dev.

'Her name is Janaki, my best friend, companion, and everything. She was staying with me the past three years after her husband demised.' Mr. Dev added.

So, he called us to introduce his new wife who wants to spend the rest of his life with. He thought and noticed a couple of his family photos in frames on either side of the huge LED television. He looked at his mother in a frame, she was smiling at him.

'How are you doing, Prabha?'

'I'm good, uncle. How are you?' Prabha said, maintaining a warm smile.

'I'm good too. But I don't know when my time ends up.'

Prasad and Prabha looked confused.

'What do you mean, dad?' Prasad asked his dad.

'Nothing. Let's go for dinner.'

Janaki arranged a dinner and called them to take a seat. They washed their hands and took their seats. In the meantime, they were still waiting for a reply from Dev. But no response to Prasad's question. They thought to not ask him the question again and completed the dinner.

They moved to the garden area following Dev and took the bean bags, provided under the beautiful hanging lights. They were still waiting for inviting after five years. Dev fired some questions at Prasad.

'When do you become an author?

'When do you keep my grandchildren in my hand?'

'Is still you were getting the haunting nightmare?'

He had to answer these questions because that was why he had been invited now. He was in awkward silence and not answered any questions of the above, there were no answers right now for the first and last questions. But the second question disappointed them as the doctors told them that she had Nulliparous.

'Nulliparous' is a medical word used to describe a woman who hasn't given birth to a child. It doesn't mean that she's never been pregnant. She had a miscarriage several times. This disappointed this couple, and his father was not aware of this news as they both hid this.

His wife slowly controlled her tears and fake smiled at them. But the last question surprised her as she was aware of his nightmare, she didn't ask him.

Dev observed them, he thought something has happened but he doesn't want to get answers right now to his questions and continued.

'I transferred all my assets into the name of my daughter-in-law Prabha, but under one condition.'

The couple glanced at Dev and asked about the condition.

'Janaki will be your family member after my demise. I mean, she will be Prasad's mom.' Dev conditioned, moved his body from the bean bag, and stood up.

They both agreed to that condition, but Prasad's face was not lit up and fake smiled.

'Do you want to sleep?' Mr. Dev asked them.

Prasad glanced at his father and then at his wife.

Janaki immediately appeared from the kitchen and escorted both Prasad and Prabha to the bedroom upstairs of the building.

6

The couple moved to the bedroom located upstairs of the building. It was a posh bedroom with expensive furniture and kept neat.

'Isn't it odd to sleep like this at someone else's place?' Prasad said, keeping his hands in his pockets.

'Hey, it's not someone else's, it's your father's before and it will be mine - ours soon.' Her wife sounded.

'I'm sorry, but I couldn't accept her as my mother.' Prasad said, removing his tee and sleeping on the bed.

Prabha understood his feeling and hugged him tightly. Prasad smiled at her and went to pee once, removed his jeans and he was in his boxer shorts.

He returned from peeing and observed her wife was not there on the bed. He looked all around the bedroom.

She entered the bedroom with a glass of milk for his husband and kept it on the table. She knew that his husband can't sleep without drinking milk at night.

'Are you still asleep?' Prabha asked him.

'Do you think I'm in the mood to talk now?' Prasad said, lifted her, and placed her on the bed.

He placed his hands on her hair and smelled and kissed it. He fingered his finger from her top of the face, and nose and paused his finger on her dry lips, to the neck, and stopped on her breasts.

'It's time to impress me,' he said and tugged down his boxers. He was kneeling on the bed while Prabha was lying on her back looking at him. Her eyes slowly went down to his manhood. She moistened her dry lips with the tip of her tongue and pushed him on the bed with her feet. She then sat on top of him, putting both her legs on either side. She removed her pink tee. As she bent down to kiss him, he unhooked her bra. She started rubbing her pelvis on his manhood, turning it even harder. He unbuttoned her jeans, unzipped them with her help, and tugged it down along with her panties. As he held his manhood, she lifted her back only to sit on it gently, allowing it to go inside her. With her hands on his chest, Prabha shut her eyes and started moving her pelvis slowly. As the initial pain of insertion slowly turned into pleasure.

Prasad flipped her and changed into the missionary position. Prabha still had her eyes shut, clutching the bed sheet tight with both hands. All her defenses were conquered by him. She opened her eyes when she felt his breath on her face. Prasad was now close to her lips. His lips pursued within no time, he took her tongue into his mouth and chewed sometimes. He squeezed her boobs with his hands and sucked on her nipples alternatively. He had increased his pace by now and she had wrapped her legs around him to escalate her pleasure. The moans became louder and louder, and they both climaxed as Prasad came inside her. Both were panting as he looked at her and said,' I love you, baby.'

'I too love you, baby.' Prabha fingering on his chest.

He kissed her and flipped her once again, holding her tight in his arms. They slept in a good position for four hours. They woke up in the morning around seven. They both sighed at each other.

'Are you hiding something from me?' She asked him.

'Yesterday, the policemen accused us as the suspects in the MK murder case.'

'Why?'

'Because We three were only asked him about the case.'

Prabha looked at him with confusion and said, 'It's okay, everything will be alright. But actually, I am not asking about this, it's about your nightmare. Why do you hide this from me?'

'I thought it will be a big trouble to you.'

'Nothing is trouble in our life. We don't hide any secrets between us.'

He was silent, she caressed his already ruffled hair. He picked up his phone and checked the notifications, and received sixteen missed calls from both Akbar and Aditya.

One text message received from Akbar: he opened and read.

'*Read today's newspaper.*'

He hurried to check the newspaper.

'What happened?' she asked him.

He showed her the text message, wearing his blue jeans and tee.

'Relax, baby.' She combed his hair with her fingers.

He went downstairs to check the newspaper, while he was searching in the living hall, Janaki understood that he was searching for a newspaper and said,' Newspaper not available, you will get in a hair salon located in front of our building.'

He didn't respond to her and ran to the hair salon and picked up the newspaper, turned the pages of the main newspaper, and then looked up in the district newspaper.

He ran to the hair salon, picked up the newspaper, turned the pages of the main newspaper, and then looked up in the district newspaper, he found tiny letters titled 'Three Suspects' and read.

Three Suspects

Date: 23/05/2022

VISAKHAPATNAM: G Raghav Sai, Superintendent of Police said, 'We caught the three suspects Prasad, Aditya, and Akbar on Monday night who might be involved in the murder case of MK alias Mohan Krishna who was recently murdered at RK Beach Road in Visakhapatnam of Andhra Pradesh on Sunday evening. Police have formed two special teams to nab the culprit.

'

An inquiry was going on and the culprit will be arrested soon.

I never expected it as we were the suspects in this murder case, especially, Since I am the main suspect in this murder case. Prasad thought to himself and moved back to the room.

He dialed Akbar and Aditya in the conference, 'We had to find the culprit, not for Fathima, it's for our three lives.'

And he ended the call, calling her wife to move on from here now.

'Okay, relax, first let's have breakfast, and then we will move.' His wife said with a warm smile.

'Okay, baby.' Prasad said.

'It's my boy.' She smiled.

He smiled back, pulled her towards him, and pinned her hands to take control of her. He was kissing his way to her navel. She somehow managed to push him away saying, 'Let's eat something first, and don't forget that we have to go home.' She could sense Prasad's eyes on her all the time. It made her blush and she turned back to move on downstairs. Prasad came from behind and scooped her up, lifting her to the bathroom and placing her under the shower. He went down on his knees, putting the tip of his tongue on her belly button. The pleasure hormones released by Prasad's touch made her feel passionate and lucky. Prasad stood up. They smooched under the cold shower.

After a prolonged fondling under the shower, they finally had breakfast with Dev and left his father's place.

While traveling on his Alto to their home, his wife asked about the text he showed her the morning.

He explained to her,' The policemen Raghav stated in the newspaper that he caught us on Monday night and projected us as the three suspects, and me as the main suspect of this murder case.'

He gazed at her, smiled, and thought,' I will write the story of the MK murder case and publish it as my debut novel for my career and fulfill my wife's desire to see me as an author.'

Prasad still had not murdered anyone or was involved in any murder case but the first time he wants to murder the police Raghav as he said that they caught them and projected them as the suspects to get only fame and medals.

He wants to become popular as an author but became a famous suspect. 'Thank God, they published only our names without any photos.' He thought to himself.

His mind was withdrawing many questions. *Who will be that murderer? What happened between the love birds in these 5 years?* Then one sudden phone call interrupted his imaginary thoughts.

8

Then one sudden phone call interrupted his imaginary thoughts.

Prasad lifted his call and said, 'Hello.'

'Hello, we are calling from the Beach Road police station. Raghav sir wants to meet you now at RK Beach Road. Don't come with your friends.' communicated someone and ended the call.

Now his mind raised more questions. *Why did the police inform me to come alone? Is Akbar or Aditya involved in this murder case? Are they both killed MK for me and my love?*

His wife interrupted and asked,' What happened?'

'The policemen called me for a small interrogation.'

They reached to their home and dropped his wife; he parked his car in parking area. Her wife thrown a bike key from the windows, he caught it and moved on his Royal Enfield to beach road.

Prasad reached Beach Road within forty-five minutes from his home.

The police Raghav was waiting for him in his jeep, wearing a maroon tee and blue jeans. He greeted him and fake smiled.

He too greeted him, moved down from the jeep, and walked on the seashore. Prasad followed him.

They walked some distance and sat on a green bench, where no crowd was visible. Raghav was silent for some time and shouted at some spicy moori mixture seller, who was passing by them.

The seller still not moved from there with some fear in his eyes, holding his cycle with moori mixture. Police walked towards him and ate it, took a bunch of papered moori mixture for Prasad to eat. The seller left the place.

Raghav moved on to the bench and given moori mixture to Prasad and said, 'Prasad, I inquired some people already about you. But now I want to listen to your whole true story in your words.'

Prasad hesitated to tell at first but when he said that he will help him to publish his debut novel. He started telling his story.

There are eight wonders in the world, but I am the first wonder to my father. He was more confused about my introverted and arrogant behavior since my childhood.

After completing my schooling in Gajuwaka, Visakhapatnam, Andhra Pradesh, I was like all the other friends who took the path of engineering. There was no decision-making involved in the choice. So, I too joined the rat race. But I know I am not interested in studies as I am passionate about writing. I always stood first place in many writing competitions and helped maximum friends in writing love letters since schooling.

'Tell me how you connected to Mohan Krishna?' the police Interrupted and questioned him.

'Wait sir, I will tell you, don't interrupt between my story,' Prasad said and continued.

I have not received good colleges as per my result in EAMCET. My father managed to purchase a management seat in Electrical and Electronics Engineering that too in one of the best engineering colleges. My mother always prayed to God to make me an engineer.

I finally landed up at GITAM Engineering College even though I know that it was what I did not want. I was accepted the same with some love and respect towards my parents.

August 2014,

GITAM COLLEGE

I joined on the third day of college and my father and I both received a warm welcome from the college reception.

'Welcome to one of the best engineering colleges in the world,' he said with a sense of pride and achievement.

I looked at my father; he was very happy with pride at the receptionist's warm welcome. And I was the first in the Galla Family to study engineering. When My father and I arrived inside the college, we have seen some students ragging freshers outside and near the canteen.

'Sir, is ragging a big problem for freshers?' my father asked the receptionist, concerned.

'Sir, you don't have to worry as the Supreme Court has declared ragging as a criminal offense and it may problem to hostellers, not to daily scholars.'

My father and I relaxed with a smile as my journey from my home to my college is approximately one hour.

After some time, when dad had about to leave me in college, I sensed his Ramayana session was about to start.

'Babu, you have to study seriously and You are at a very crucial stage of life. You have to handle your life yourself from now onwards. Some friends will change your behavior. No Cigarettes, no alcohol, no bad friends, and no girlfriends! We belong to a middle-class family, and you have to think about money in every spending.'

Babu was my nickname. I was surprised by his words as he was leaving me suddenly in an ocean. I have to return home by evening 6 p.m. But his words made me feel emotional but at the same time I want to tell him that don't keep any hope in me as I was not interested in studies, I want to become a writer.

'Ok Dad, 'I nodded, although I knew I would not follow any of his instructions. He was unstoppable with his Ramayana sessions and finally left for Gajuwaka.

That morning around ten, I entered my classroom to find many new faces. I met Akbar.

'Hi, I am Muhammad Akbar from Gajuwaka.'

'Hello, I am Prasad from Gajuwaka.'

Akbar frowned, 'Just Prasad?'

'Oh, it's Prasad Babu Galla.'

In our locality, people may forget their first name, but no surname. We both became closer friends as we were belonging to the same place even not the same religion.

Before I introduce my enemies, let me introduce all my friends as my story revolves around these people.

Muhammad Akbar: We both came from the same town. He was a simple Muslim guy who follow his traditional riots. His favorite actor was Amir Khan. He had a big following in the political field as his father was a political activist.

Suresh Kumar Sahoo: He was from Bhubaneswar, Orissa. He was very talkative in the unknown Telugu language and very confident. He never gives anyone to talk with him. Everyone must listen to his words.

Aditya Ram: He was a master at scanning girls from top to bottom. I can't even bear to mention the kind of things he would find out about girls even you can't find on Google. He was a master at talking to girls with no hesitation. He was very thin, smart, and handsome too.

Now let me introduce my enemies, actually not that much conversation between us, you will know how they were my enemies.

Mohan Krishna: He was our class topper and class representative. He can't live a single day without complaining about me. He was six feet tall, a broad bodybuilder, intelligent, and very handsome. Anyone can fall in love with him.

Keshav Raj: He was not a topper and irregular to college but no party will be organized without him. His college attendance will manage by his rich dad.

Sanjay Kumar: He was a thin, innocent, and simple guy. He was loved by everyone in college. He was a musician at our college events.

I don't understand why minimum girls join in Electrical and Mechanical branches. I discovered that beautiful girls join in only CSE and IT branches. Every day we were watching those minimum girls, actually only seven girls in our class. I found only one beautiful girl that too a Muslim girl.

'Then your love story begins,' the police interrupted again as he was involved deep in the story.

'Don't know, it's love or not. I called it Love.'

9

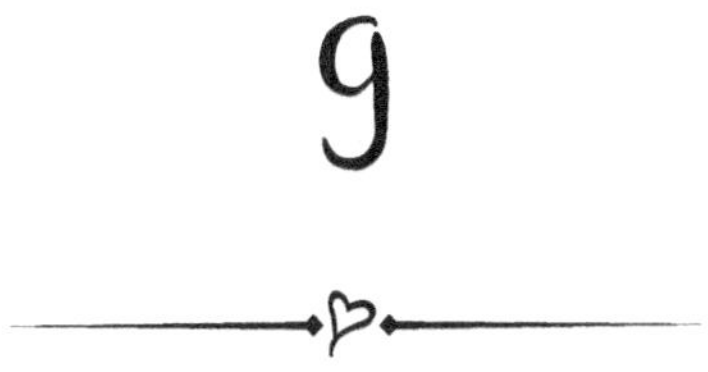

Prasad continued his story.

Suddenly and surprisingly, some group of half a dozen gregarious men entered our room, shouting like military men. 'Every boy must stand up on the bench and girls have to introduce themselves including Sir at the end.'

I remembered the words of the receptionist as he said no ragging problem for day scholars. There may be any special treatment for boys and some concessions for girls. We all stood on the bench with some shivering. Some seniors searched all our pockets and looted like dacoits.

I rewind my dad's words,' *You have to think about money in every spending.*' But Dad, I am not spending, some dacoits looting, said myself internally.

Boys, meet our afternoon in the canteen and give us treat whatever we want to eat, one of the seniors shouted in a horrible voice.

I started staring at them like a prisoner waiting for food in jail. One of the seniors observed my staring and shouted,' Why were you staring like a hero? Come with me now.'

Akbar raised his voice,' Why does he have to come with you?' I looked at Akbar with some surprise, at how he raised his voice against these dacoits. Then senior shouted, 'You also come with me.'

But we were not moved a single inch and one of the seniors slowly said, 'This is not ragging, it's just an introduction.'

The dacoits cooled and let all boys sit. Then they asked the seven girls to say their names and every boy was gazing at the girls to know their names.

Out of seven, I heard a sweet voice from a beautiful girl, 'My name is Fathima, from MVP Colony, Visakhapatnam.'

Fathima was very thin, tall, and fair, her high cheekbones gave her face a strange charm, her skin glowed, and she was wearing a light pink gloss on her thin lips. Her hair was the boyish cut that delicately framed her face. I also took in her delicate neck and the way her top hugged her breasts, flowing over her flat belly. My eyes had lingered I could see the jeans meeting the top. The first time I explored a girl like this and want to explore some more. I was almost opened my mouth and starved for wildness. I imagined her in doing blowjob with me and suddenly someone interrupted my imagination. It was Mohan Krishna.

'So, you murdered him for this.' Police again interrupted.

'Sir, Why I kill him for this silly reason?'

'Then you murdered him for another reason!'

'Sir, I have not murdered him. Let me continue my story.'

'Okay, continue.'

Prasad again continued his story.

'When will the ragging end?' Mohan Krishna asked.

A senior came to Mohan and shouted,' Listen, juniors, this is not ragging! it's training! It will end after the fresher's party.'

After a few days, our freshers' party and ragging both ended. Seniors became our friends and we enjoyed their motivation. Our playboy, Aditya not stopped scanning our senior girls too and they also enjoyed his presence. Suresh and Akbar started teasing every girl from other branches also. I too followed them to gaze at the girls and we ranked them as per their curvy bodies, fairness, and sizes of breasts.

After the late-night Ramayana sessions with my dad, I woke up early in the morning and reached the college in a fresh mood to enjoy gazing at beauty. This day was different and amazing.

'When your love story begins.' The police interrupted again.

'Now, I was going to tell that only.'

That day, at around 09:20 a.m., our seven girls entered the classroom. My eyes gazed only at Fathima; with my mouth opened like a crocodile and water running from it. The first time, I felt why girls and boys sit apart.

I settled in between Akbar and Aditya, in the wild hope of staring at Fathima. I noticed her from top to bottom, wearing stylish spectacles, dark green Kurtis, and light green salwar.

'Good morning, sir,' everyone screamed in unison.

'Good morning, students,' the professor replied.

A thin, normal height, dark-colored professor and curly hair entered with a fake killer smile. We can't see his dark face as we can see only his whitish teeth. With his normal build, gold wristwatch, gold chain on his neck, and green canvas shoes, Professor Rajesh looked like a goldsmith. After taking attendance, Rajesh sir wrote 'Electrical Engineering' on the board with white chalk. He started taking classes but no one was listening. His voice was very thin as a small girl's. Our entire class smiled mischievously. Mr. Rajesh noticed and stopped teaching, shouting, and left the class.

Aditya whispered,' Babu, Mohan Krishna was also gazing at her like a hungry poor boy waiting for a food packet in floods.'

I observed Mohan Krishna, yes, Aditya was right. He was gazing at her. I thought MK was a competitor for me.

After noticing Fathima's smile, I became an instant fan of her smile. But after watching Mohan, my blood boiled like a pressure cooker. I mumbled myself, *'Babu, please stay within your limits. You should not develop any crush and that too she is a Muslim girl.'*

I was reminded of my father's words, *no girlfriends.* I thought to myself, *I don't love anyone, I don't need any girlfriend, but I can't stop loving Fathima.*

'So, you loved Fathima but they loved each other, then you planned and murdered MK.' Raghav confirmed.

10

Raghav confirmed that Prasad murdered MK.

Prasad interrupted the declaration of the police, saying, he was not a murderer and continued his story.

We had C Programming Lab after a few days. Laboratory classes in Engineering were a big opportunity for students to spend time together for maximum hours. The boys could flirt with their targets. As my roll number was not near to my target, I felt disgusted when my enemy's roll number was next to my target.

I'd expressed my desire to interact and sit with Fathima in class but we have to sit according to roll numbers. Mohan Krishna and Fathima sat together on the same bench, which made me more egoist. They were talking and smiling at each other, which I can't tolerate anymore. My thoughts were like killing him in the same class. Then some annoying voice halted my thoughts.

'Do you have any doubts, Mr. Prasad?' Anisha asked, making herself as if she was one of the most intelligent persons in the class.

Anisha, was a minimum thin girl, an average student, a tall girl, her face was smooth but lacked softness. Her high cheekbones accentuated her narrow chin, broad sturdy shoulders, and long hands with bony. The steady dark eyes under her shapely brows and overall nice appearance but not as much beauty as Fathima. Moreover, I was thinking about Fathima even I sit beside Anisha. I can pay attention to her even from a distance.

Love has no religion. I don't know why I have fallen in love with her. That was my first love.

A year passed, and now we became seniors. Aditya, Akbar, and I were very exciting and busy searching for junior beauties. Maybe you were thinking that I forgot to mention another friend Suresh. He left the college as his father was transferred to Kolkata.

We decided to rag even after freshers' party, not like our seniors. Every junior finds their first college function exciting similar to us. We would be heroes searching for new girlfriends and would explore any part of the beauties.

Our class is divided into two gangs: Babu Gang and MK (Mohan Krishna) gang. After knowing Fathima and MK were love in with each other, I was disturbed a lot and I explored new and weird habits such as Alcohol, cigarettes, girlfriends, and fights. Everything changed within me after my heart broke but not my love for Fathima.

Akbar, Aditya, and I organized a freshers' party with our opposite gang as this was our prestigious first event.

We had been shortlisted two boys Deepak, Ajay, and two girls Meena, Sonia among ten boys and ten girls from juniors for the final round of the Mr. and Mrs. Fresher contest from our batch.

We were happy because we shortlisted two beautiful girls and we would rag them every day to make them our new girlfriends. They both performed very well in dance competitions.

Aditya, our scanner already scanning them from top to bottom without leaving an inch. Akbar was busy ragging boys and looting their wallets. We three were like dacoits with weird beards.

'You both were quite impressive,' I said to these beauties.

'Thank you, sir.' both replied.

'You had to meet me after half an hour in our Library,' I said.

'Why, sir?' she replied with some shivering.

'Don't question, seniors. We, seniors.' I shouted at her.

'Okay, sir.' she panicked.

I believe that every human being has two sides to their personality. One is good and the other is bad. One side is Angel and one side is demons. I started changing into a demon after my heart was broken. I was trying to hide my desire, but the demon inside me came out when I saw Meena and Sonia. I guess, there is something wrong with my mind but I can't control my desire.

It was quiet in the library around 8 p.m. and the end of the fresher's party. Meena was sitting on the chair, waiting for me in the silence between the books. I entered into the room with great excitement. She stood from the chair and managed a fake smile on her red cheeks. I moved very closer to her and brushed her hair with my tip of fingers, slowly touched her cheeks. She was shivering and her eyes slowly went down and my manhood raging very hard rock. She moistened her dry lips when I touched her lips with my tip of a finger. My manhood forcing me to do sex. I pushed her on the table and I sat on the top of her, putting both my legs on either side. She removed her tee and I bent down to kiss her. She unhooked her bra and I seduced her breasts. I unbuttoned her jeans, unzipped it with her help, pulled down her panties. I held my penis, suddenly searched for the condom but she held it and popped into her mouth, moving in and out. I ended the world war as the angel inside me stopped and worn our clothes. I smiled at her and dropped her at her home.

The next day morning, Akbar countered,' You were performing well in the library too.' It's not you, It's a demon within you. Be you, as an angle as you were before.

I was silent with his words and rewind my father's words,' *No Cigarettes, no alcohol, no bad friends, and no girlfriends!*' I felt bad and tears dropped out of my eyes.

We, Seniors, but it should be up to some limit. I concentrated on my studies but I know it was not possible. So, I became a writer in college, was writing love stories for our college magazines and was appreciated by everyone including Fathima and MK gang.

Two years passed and we completed our graduation. Fathima scored top in our college and next to her, was Mohan Krishna. Millions of questions, how do love birds can study well without any disturbance. Some of my classmates got selected in campus selections.

I was listening to daily Ramayana sessions by my dad for not getting a job in campus selections. Every day I was hiding my face from my father. But one night, my father did not wake up and wait for me before TV when I entered the home and started his usual Ramayana session.

'Babu, you have to do a job and make us proud. No one studied engineering in our family. We belong to a middle-class family, and you have to be the best son.'

I was surprised by his words. I expected that he will be angry with me. He had never had an opportunity to study as a professional. His words made me feel emotional but at the same time, I felt overburdened by them. I know we are financially weak. But I don't know how I will be the best son.

'Ok dad,' I nodded in response.

After this session, he left for his room.

That night at around eleven, I entered my room after dinner. I thought for some time and decided to follow my passion.

The next morning, my dad was sitting on a balcony taking a fresh wind, reading a newspaper in one hand, and taking a sip of hot tea. I came out of my room and I thought it would be the best time – since I had nothing to do other than writing. I could spend my time as I wanted but everything changed that one morning.

'Dad, I have decided to become a writer,' said in a low tone.

'Writer?' my dad said in frustration.

'Yes Dad, I would love to write books,' I added.

'I am fixing your marriage soon with your Geetha auntie's daughter, then your career might change.' said angered.

'Da...d, Da...d, What the hell is?' I was about to faint and remained silent.

I don't know how my career change after marriage. If my mom will be there, she might agree with my decision.

'I miss you mom and I love you mom,' I memorized by seeing her collage on a wall.

After my mother's demise, Geetha auntie sister of my father promised my dad that they marry her daughter to me. She pampered me and always care about my well-being. Initially, I thought it was her caring, but later I realized she want to marry her daughter with me. It seemed like she was waiting for this to happen.

When dad was struggling at his job end, Geetha Auntie and her husband helped financially. So, I remained silent and agreed that I marry her but I needed some time to settle in my career. Suddenly dad blasted a bomb into my life with his frustrating decision.

So, that day my father presented an unexpected gift.

Finally, we got engaged and married within a week.

So, again after five years, we heard MK'S name as a dead man in the newspaper. This was the true story.

The police listened his story but he was just staring at him in silent killing mode.

And then he announced to leave now and be ready to cooperate for further investigation.

Prasad left the police station and reached his home on his Royal Enfield around evening six.

He rang the doorbell, his wife opened and hugged him.

Prabha looked up at him and said softly, 'I'm scared, Baby.'

Prasad hugged her tighter.

He cooled her by kissing on her forehead and asked, 'Now tell me what happened?'

'Nothing, I felt alone and slept, I dreamt a bad nightmare.'

Prasad smiled at her and said, 'My nightmares haunting you now.'

She smiled back and said, 'What way you end your nightmare?'

'Akbar and me, going tomorrow to meet the famous Psychiatrist Mr. Chowdhury.'

He dialed Akbar from his mobile and informed him to book an appointment for tomorrow.

'I already informed him; we will go tomorrow night around eight to his home.' Akbar communicated.

Akbar received a call from an unknown number.

'Okay, dude, I am getting a call, I will talk to you later. Bye, bye.' He ended the call.

Prasad and Prabha had dinner and left to their bedroom.

11

The next morning, Prasad woke up morning around four forty-five and he meditated, went jogging and returned back around six. His thoughts were all about the policemen and the murder case.

It might be his plan to use suspects to find the real culprit. *I was helping, not just for me, my friends were also helping the police to find the murderer.* He thought.

The Police, G. Raghav Sai was a sincere police officer, with a sharp eye, above 6' feet taller, a heavy loudspeaker voice, and a steel cage body. He was awarded several times as the best police officer by Andhra Pradesh government. He was a terror to every criminal, gangster, and even politician also.

Prasad watched about him several times on Television as he encountered many criminals and solved many murder cases within twenty-four hours but this murder case was delaying. These three friends were cooperating the police in the investigation and the first time everyone was surprising that he formed two special teams to find the murderer.

I think something was going on around this murder case, I still can't understand what's happening why this murder case was delayed. Prasad closed his eyes and thinking, sitting on the giant sofa in the living hall.

Prasad phone was vibrating, but he had not seen as he kept in silent mode. He was still thinking about the police: *Is he good or bad?*

He felt someone touched his shoulder, he opened his eyes slowly, it was his beautiful wife. His thoughts were interrupted by her, holding a special cup of coffee made by love. He smiled at her and held a cup, sipped a coffee.

The phone was still ringing, she picked up and said,' hey, a call from your dad, received eleven missed calls.'

'Leave it, I don't want to talk with him. I had my problems already, now he created another problem.'

'Baby, he had written already all his assets in my name. Is it a problem to you?'

'That's not my problem, Problem is Janaki.'

'Baby, leave it, that's not a problem, I will handle it. First you lift the call and hear what he says.'

'Okay, baby, as you said.' He picked up his mobile from his wife and lifted the call.

'Hello, dad.'

'Hi my son, how are you? I heard that you were a main suspect in the MK murder case. How it would be? If you had to share anything with me, just share with me. I will not reveal it to anyone.'

'Dad! Nothing to share, it's just a piece of false news from the police. Maybe he was doing it for fame, medals, or promotions. I am also inquiring from my side to find the murderer but have not gotten any clues up to now. I will find that culprit.'

'Okay, Babu, be aware of the police Raghav also, I heard that he was not a good man and don't involve more in this murder case.'

'Ok, dad. I will manage this, you no need to worry. Take care of your Janaki.'

Prasad's harsh words disappointed him, and he ended the call.

Prasad thrown his mobile on the couch and started thinking again about the police. *What's the story of the police? Is he the Demon or an angel?*

Prasad showered, had breakfast and went to the university library on his bike, collected all the old newspapers, read the news about him. But nowhere he found him as a demon.

He called Akbar and informed that he was researching about Raghav, nowhere he found him as a bad police officer.

On that day evening around six, Prasad met Akbar and raised that he had some suspicious doubts on the police Raghav.

'I found different news about Mr. Raghav on the same newspaper 'Praja Sakthi' by the same reporter but I don't know if it's true or not.' Akbar informed.

'Really! What's that?'

'Headline: The Corrupted Police: created another income source.' Akbar read loudly and continued.

The Corrupted Police: created another income source
Date: 15/04/2010

VIJAYAWADA: G Raghav Sai, Sub Inspector of Police caught red-handed by our reporter Joseph while taking a bribe from one of the farmers who came to complain to the bank manager Arvind Swamy for torturing him to clear the loans as soon as possible.

Somehow Raghav managed the farmer not to complain against him and said, 'This was just a piece of false allegation, I am not corrupted and never encourage any corruption.'

Our reporter says this was not the first time he was corrupted; he was a corrupted officer who created another income source to build his dream house and to buy jewelry for his wife.

Fake encounter by Rowdy Police

Date: 22/05/2010

VISAKHAPATNAM: G Raghav Sai, Sub Inspector of Police (Rowdy Police) fake encounter with the Maoists but they were not real Maoists. They were the students of the tribal area at Chintapalli of Visakhapatnam.

The police officials said,' we caught the Maoists in the forest area who were trying to kill the policemen by placing bombs in various places near that forest area. We recognized nearly 30 bombs and 20 different types of guns and bullets.'

Our reporter says that he was a fake encounter specialist. He killed many innocent tribal students in the name of Maoists to get fame and promotions.

Akbar continued reading aloud from his massive collection of newspapers.

Is he police or criminal?

Date: 22/05/2010

VISAKHAPATNAM: G Raghav Sai, Sub Inspector of Police and criminal who interrogated the rape case of 23-year-old tribal woman Manisha, closed the case by arresting the innocent tribal man Gangadhar by keeping false allegations to support one of the local politician's son JM Reddy, who kidnapped and raped her.

The police officials said,' we caught rapist Gangadhar who brutally raped Manisha yesterday at Radha Krishna wines. There was a false allegation against the innocent man JM Reddy just for sake of money as he was the rich politician's son.'

Our reporter says that Raghav was corrupted by criminal police supporting the politician's son by taking bribes from the rich and closing the case.

Akbar started reading another headline, Prasad interrupted him and said, 'Stop reading buddy, we have to meet him and ask him about this. How can he solve this MK Murder case?'

'First we have to meet the reporter Joseph and collect more proofs against the police.'

'Akbar! No matter whether the police were bad or good, we need to solve this murder case and find the murderer.'

'Ok then, let's meet Raghav, the bad police.'

On that day evening, they both met Raghav in his office and asked about all the news that they read in the newspaper collection.

'Have you found all this news published in any other newspapers? No, right. Because this all news was published against me by only one reporter Joseph, who falsely allegation by him. This all news published was not true.' The police informed them.

'How can I believe you that you solve this case by finding the real culprit? We will meet the reporter today itself and know the truth.' Prasad said in frustration.

'He was no more. He killed himself by feeling guilty, which means he made suicide after knowing that he published false news about me.'

'I heard that you solve every case within twenty-four hours without forming any team. But in this case, you formed two special teams and why this murder case was still delaying.'

'I had some personal family issues so that I decided to spare some time for my family and then I formed two special teams to not burden myself. So that this case may be delayed but I will find culprit as soon as possible.'

Akbar and Prasad were confused to know which was true, Is he bad or good?

When they were leaving the police station, the police interrupted Akbar and said, 'Akbar! Don't forget that your interrogation on tomorrow morning. Come around morning ten.'

They both moved to parking area. Akbar picked up his mobile to check the time. It was eight already.

Akbar remembered Prasad about the appointment with his uncle Chowdhury. Now it's already 8:30 p.m.

They both reached to Chowdhury's home around 9 p.m., It's not a house, it's a palace,' Prasad said, by seeing Chowdhury's house from outside.

'How much he will charge from one patient?' he added.

'It's almost three to four lakhs.'

'What! I can't afford that much.'

'He will not charge anything from us.'

'Then, Okay.'

They both moved near to the gate and parked outside the gate, and called the security guard.

The security guard opened the long gate and greeted both of them.

'Hello Akbar Sir! Chowdhury sir was calling you since evening around six. Your phone was not reachable.' He added.

'What! My phone was not reachable, maybe there was no signal in the police station.' Akbar responded.

'Is Chowdhury sir not there in home?' Prasad asked.

'Yes sir, he was not there. He got an emergency call of his son from U.S.A. So, his son booked flight at 7:30 p.m. So that he called you many times but your phone was not reachable.' The security guard said pointing his finger at Akbar.

'Can you tell me U.S.A contact number?' Akbar asked.

'I don't know sir as his son calls us to the landline number.'

'Okay, when will he return?'

'Maybe after two months only.'

Prasad kept his face very dull and he had not expected this. Akbar observed his face and said, 'No problem, dude, just two months, everything will be alright then.'

'Hmm, it's okay, let's move on.'

'So, tomorrow is your interrogation.' he added.

'Yes, dude, we have to come out of this as soon as possible.'

They both left the place and Prasad dropped at Akbar's home.

Prasad's wife still waiting for him, sitting on the couch and changing channels on the television with remote. She heard the footsteps somewhere; she muted the television and listened the sound of the footsteps again to know where it was coming from. Her heartbeat was moving speed rather than normal. She picked up her mobile and dialled her husband, but his mobile was switched off.

The footsteps approaching near to their flat sounded more now, she was muted and sat silently on couth with some fear. The door was knocked but she hesitated to open. She moved at the door, again someone knocked the door and she felt diffidence. She stood at the door, then again someone knocked the door saying, 'Hey baby, open the door.' It was Prasad. she relaxed, opened the door and hugged him very tightly. She looked at his face and cried.

He hugged her and kissed on her forehead. He understood her fear and calmed her. He showered, both had dinner and she slept in his arms the whole night.

12

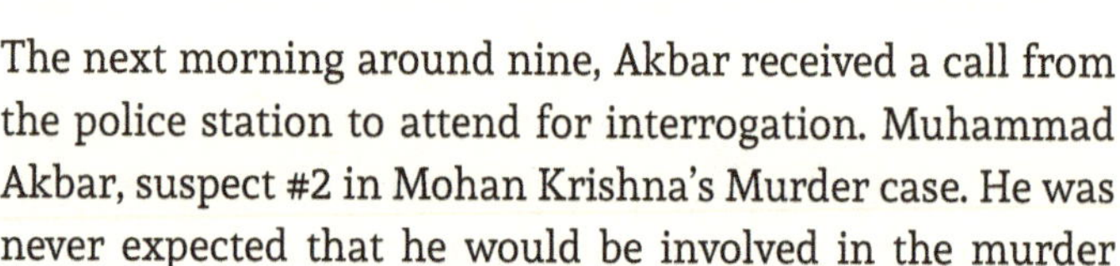

The next morning around nine, Akbar received a call from the police station to attend for interrogation. Muhammad Akbar, suspect #2 in Mohan Krishna's Murder case. He was never expected that he would be involved in the murder case.

Is Raghav the bad police officer? Is he projected them as the main suspects to divert the case? Every question will be answered until they found the real story behind this murder case.

When Akbar heard that MK was murdered, his heart weighed more than normal even though he had not that much connected to him. After reading the news, he called his best friend Prasad to share the news. At once he had suspected Prasad as a murderer as he said that he would kill Mohan Krishna anytime. He thought Prasad planned and murdered him without knowing them but still, they want to confirm. So, these three friends met on the day and confirmed he was not murdered.

'We trapped in this case by meeting the police on that night by just listening to the words of Prabha, my friend Prasad's wife.' He thought to himself.

It was morning around ten-thirty, Akbar reached the police station and met the police in his office.

The police interrogation started with the same routine questions. Akbar answered all his questions without any hesitation and continued his story.

My name is Muhammad Akbar. My father's name is Muhammad Sheik Abdul and my Mother's name is Muhammad Farah. I was only one son to them, born in a middle-class family. My father was a political activist and my mother was a housewife.

I joined GITAM engineering college after completing my schooling in Gajuwaka, Visakhapatnam, Andhra Pradesh.

On the third day of my college, I observed one father giving preaching to his son in the corridor of our college, saying, *'Babu, you have to study seriously and You are at a very crucial stage of life. You have to handle your life yourself from now onwards. Some friends will change your behavior. No Cigarettes, no alcohol, no bad friends, and no girlfriends! We belong to a middle-class family, and you have to think about money in every spending.'*

He nodded to his dad's words and I left from there by smiling myself and remembered my Abbu's words.

'All fathers were same.' I said to myself.

That morning around ten, I entered my classroom to find many new faces. Sometimes later I met the same guy whom I have seen at corridor listening to his dad's preaching.

I took initiative to make him as my friend and introduced myself, 'Hi, I am Muhammad Akbar from Gajuwaka.'

'Hello, I am Prasad from Gajuwaka,' he replied.

I asked,' Just Prasad?'

'Oh, it's Prasad Babu Galla.' he replied with a bubbly smile on his red cheeks.

We both became closer friends as we were belonging to the same place and on the same day, I met Suresh Kumar Sahoo and Aditya Ram who became very close friends.

Our other classmates Mohan Krishna, Keshav Raj and Sanjay Kumar were opposite to us as we had different opinions and tastes. We were unable to close to their hearts for making friends. So, we were very far from them.

We had only seven girls in our class. They may not be an angel but we don't have any option to watch them.

In the first year, we were ragged by our seniors but we became friends with them after our fresher's party.

I observed that Prasad, every day and every moment stared Fathima who was the only one beautiful girl in our class. I thought at first he's just staring but he said that he was in love with her. So, we promised to help him.

One day in our Electrical Class Aditya whispered,' Babu, Mohan Krishna was also gazing at her like a hungry poor boy waiting for a food packet in floods.'

Then Prasad and I noticed Mohan Krishna, yes, Aditya was right. He was gazing at her.

Mohan Krishna and Fathima were very closer day by day, smiling, talking and sharing their tiffin boxes each other as his roll number was next to her. They sat together on the same bench in every lab as per their roll numbers. They both were absenting on the same day. We were confused first and we understood that they were in love together but we were silent somedays.

A year passed, and now we became seniors but our close friend Suresh left our college as his dad was transferred to Kolkata, but he was in contact with us. We ragged our juniors especially girls.

On the fresher's day night, I observed Prasad was going to library with Meena, one of the junior girls. But as we were in hurry after the party, Aditya and I left the college that day.

On the next day morning, I heard that Prasad and Meena had sex together. My anger doubled and countered him,' You were performing well in the library too.' It's not you, It's a demon within you. Be you, as an angle as you were before.

He was silent with no words and cried aloud by hugging me and he told,' I love Fathima very much but we know that MK and Fathima loved each other. To forget her, I was doing these mischievous things.'

'To forget her, this was not the right thing. Follow your passion to become success in your life.' I explained him.

Then he started studying well and followed his passion of writing. He was a famous writer in our college and published his short novels in our college magazines. He was appreciated by everyone including Fathima and MK gang.

Third Year, fourth year, he studied well but he still loved Fathima.

On the last day of Farewell party, morning around six, my phone was ringing and I opened my eyes on bed, it was a call from Prasad. I lifted and said,' Hello,' in sleepy voice.

'Good morning, Today I want to propose Fathima.'

'Good morning, dude, at last, you took good decision but first, we have to warn him.'

'This evening we will meet him. Tell Aditya to arrange a meeting with him.' Prasad ended his call.

I put my mobile on my bed and slept again. After an hour, I woke up and showered.

I had my breakfast and dialled Aditya, informed him to arrange a meeting with Mohan Krishna today evening.

'Okay, my dear friend.' Aditya communicated.

I like Aditya because he never questions more as he understood our intentions and feelings.

Prasad arrived my home around morning ten, sounding horn, I came out of my home and moved to the Alpha Restaurant. We ordered the spicy chicken fry biriyani with starter of chilly prawns. We both chilled our maximum time there and left to college around evening four for our farewell party.

That evening Aditya arranged a meeting with Mohan Krishna at their college canteen.

Prasad shouted at him and said, 'Hey, how dare you get closer to my girlfriend.'

I said, 'From today, you shouldn't talk or be around her.'

Aditya advised him, 'She is our Babu's girlfriend, be far from her, otherwise you don't know what will happen to you further.'

Mohan Krishna said, 'I can't understand whom you are talking about.'

Then Aditya mumbled, 'Don't act smart buddy, we were talking about Fathima.'

'Is she Babu's girlfriend? Does she know that?'

I interrupted and said, 'Babu will propose to her today, so you better keep away from her.'

Mohan Krishna chuckled loudly and declared, 'We have been in love with each other since our first year of college.'

We all knew that they love each other but acted like we don't know at all.

Prasad warned him, 'Whatever happened till now, leave it, she is mine now... She......is......mine.......now.'

Mohan Krishna angered on Prasad and knocked a shot on his cheeks, it became tomato red. We dragged him back to save his life from MK.

We left the place and moved to our homes.

After a week, we received our results, we passed and completed our graduation. Fathima scored top in our college and next to her, was Mohan Krishna. They also got selected in campus selections.

As I was interested in business, I started cement traders' business and continuing till now.

I was not in contact with MK and his friends but after five years, I heard that MK and Fathima were going to marry soon. And some days later, I have seen MK Murder case in newspaper. We three met that day and came to police station to meet you for collecting details to help Prasad to make him as a debut author.

The police interrupted and asked, 'Where were you on the day of murder?'

'I invited my friend Prasad and his wife Prabha for lunch to my house, so we were in my home up to evening and then I went to his house for dinner that night.'

'Ok, you can leave now. I will call you again.'

'Sir, interrogate as quick as possible, I had business to do. I can't come again and again.'

'Already case will be on going, you have to cooperate with us.' the police said in low tone.

Akbar was surprised as the police first time; he was not shouted at him. He was speaking very calmly like the peaceful Buddha. He left the police station with a confused state of mind.

13

The following day, Akbar dialed Prasad and informed about how the interrogation happened. They both communicated just a normal talk and Akbar ended call as he received an important call from his cement dealers.

On the same day, Aditya received a call from the police station to come for interrogation. Everyone thinks that he was a play boy in his college but he actually acted like a play boy just to show off. He was an innocent man, always thinks about his family and two friends.

It was around ten, he reached to the police station. He still doesn't understand why and how they were trapped in MK murder case.

'I enjoyed my life by scanning girls in our college but now what's happened to my life, they were scanning me whenever I entered into the police station.' He thought himself while entering into police station.

He was looking around in the police station, some prisoners looking at him like man eaters, if they were out, definitely he will be out.

One of the constables said,' Hello Aditya, Sir was inside his cabin, waiting for you. Go, go fast.'

'Okay, sir.

Aditya entered and stood at entrance of Raghav's cabin with his shivering body. He was still had some fear whenever he was nearby to Raghav. He looked the Police's face; it was like a serious killer looking to hunt him.

The police saw Aditya and said in a serious tone, 'Yes, come in, Mr. Aditya. Have a seat now?'

Aditya slowly took his chair and said, Thank you, sir.' He was astonished by his warm welcome into the cabin.

'Hello Aditya, your both friends told me everything without keeping any secret from the first scene of how you met and become friends and the last scene of how and why you met me at police station.'

'They told everything!' he exclaimed.

'Yes, they said everything including the scene of your last day in college.'

'Okay sir, I will tell you everything.'

Aditya started his story.

My name is Manchu Aditya Ram. My dad's name is Manchu Sri Ram and mom's name is Manchu Seetha. I had one brother Manchu Rana and one sister Manchu Sakshi.

The police shouted at him, 'Shut up! This Manchu nonsense and come into the main story.'

He was scared and continued his story.

My father was working as Real Estate broker. He joined me in GITAM college after completing my schooling.

I am an average student passed in EAMCET examination and I didn't get the engineering seat in best college. So, my father purchased a management seat in Electrical and Electronics Engineering. Even my dad knows about my poor studies but need some degree to get a job.

I joined the third day of college and followed some fee procedure, after that my father left from the college.

That morning around 10:20 a.m., I entered into my classroom to find many new faces. The two men shaking hands at the middle row of middle bench. I too joined them and took initiative to make friends. We started our conversation talking about our studies, girls, Cricket and more. Then suddenly another Oriya guy interrupted our conversation and introduced himself as Suresh.

I had some weakness of girls, just to talk with them but not any other intention. I had some skill of scanning girls from top to bottom, no matter what their color be.

Prasad had some attraction or it may be desire towards Fathima but he was thinking that it's a true love.

One day morning, I observed that Mohan Krishna was also gazing her, so informed to Prasad and Akbar. Prasad emotionally angered himself as a pressure cooker.

After some days, MK and Fathima closed each other. They can't interact and smile each other. They used to sit on the same bench in labs, canteens, under trees, libraries, no place left everywhere around and around. Sometimes both were absent on the same day. Some gossips, art and their names with symbol of love on the library walls, canteen walls and even in washrooms. These things make Prasad unbearable; his patience was uncontrollable and he became weird day by day.

In our second year, Prasad explored new and weird habits of the Alcohol, cigarettes, girls, and fights. Everyone knows that Fathima and MK both were in love each other, but they act like only friends in college.

The first time, I have seen other side of Prasad's personality. I saw him as a villain, a good villain with bad personality. I was never thought he would be romance with girls. I thought myself that he was not in love with Fathima. It's just a desire.

Everyone knows in our college that Prasad had sex with Meena, our junior on the night of freshers' day. Then how can a girl love him if he was a demon, especially how

Fathima love him.

Surprisingly, he changed his character and became a good magazine writer of our college within our last three years of college.

The last day of our college morning around eight, I received a phone call from Akbar to arrange a special meeting with MK. I lifted his call and communicated.

'Akbar, what's going on?'

'Prasad wants to propose Fathima today.'

'Okay.'

I have not questioned anything.

It's good thing but MK and Fathima were in love. Prasad also knows that, how he will propose her. I thought to myself.

I searched for contact of MK in my contact's list. I found his number, dialled him and he lifted my call.

'Hello, Mohan Krishna, this is Aditya, your classmate.'

'Hello, Aditya, I had your contact already. It's very surprised, you called me!'

I smiled and said, 'This evening, we want to talk with you at our college canteen.'

'What about?'

'You will know by that time. We will see you this evening, Bye, bye.'

I ended the call, had my lunch and spend that afternoon with my family. Then I reached the college evening around four for farewell party.

The conversation started at our college canteen between Mk and us.

Prasad shouted at him, 'Hey, how dare you get closer to my girlfriend.'

Akbar warned him, 'From today, you shouldn't talk or be around her.'

I advised him 'She is our Babu's girlfriend, be far from her, otherwise you don't know what will happen to you further.'

The police interrupted him and said, Oh! This is warning. Okay, continue.'

Mohan Krishna said, 'I can't understand whom you are talking about.'

'Don't act smart buddy, you know that we were talking about Fathima,' I mumbled.

'Is she Babu's girlfriend? Does she know that?'

Akbar interrupted and said, 'Babu will propose to her today, so you better keep away from her.'

Mohan Krishna smiled and said, 'We have been in love with each other since our first year.'

Prasad warned him, 'Whatever happened till now, leave it, she is mine now... She......is......mine.......now.'

Mohan Krishna knocked a shot on his cheeks and we pulled him back to save his life from MK.

'Your death is in my hands. Save your life from me. I don't know when I will kill you.' Prasad shouted while we moving back.

We left the place and reached 'Durga Bar and Restaurant.' We ordered three large Kingfisher Strong Beers and a Spicy Onion Chips packet.

We completed the first round, then the second, and finally the third round.

'Will...... you kill...... him really?' I inquired.

'Hush.... don't reveal...... outside. I will pl....an and kill that bloody lover. Does he snatch Fathima away from me?' Prasad said in an intoxicant bang.

Where's this beard and weird man, Ak......bar? Prasad asked me.

I pointed my finger behind the table, he was already sleeping under the table intoxicated and we both too followed him.

After five years, I heard the name of MK in the newspaper that he was murdered.

'Sir, this was the story. Please consider and state that we were not any suspects.' Aditya requested the police.

'Okay man, I will consider and call the journalists to state that you and Aditya were not any suspects but not Prasad.'

'Why not Prasad?'

'As per your statement, MK was killed by Prasad as he warned, planned very well in these five years and finally murdered MK. But anyhow until our special teams finalise the real culprit, Prasad was a main suspect.'

'The police man played his game very well with me by stating that they told everything. But we know that we were just suspects not murderers. He mumbled himself.

He came out of the hell, police station from the Yama Raja, the police Raghav around evening four and walked a mile to the parking area where he parked his bike. He picked up his mobile from his pocket, dialled Prasad and informed everything what happened in the police station.

14

That day evening, Prasad slowly sipping a special coffee, watching Pawan Kalyan movie 'KUSHI' on TV Channel raised full volume even though he was not his favorite actor, eating tasty onion pakora made by his cute darling.

'Pakora will be tasty as it was made by my sweet heart even, I found oilier.' He thought himself and said, 'Pawan Kalyan movies were watchable especially for this movie with a life partner.'

They both were eating, watching TV and talking about the murder case, his first book, second book, third book, royalties and money savings.

'I am very lucky as you were not talking about sarees, jewelries, hand bags, and footwear. Maybe you're more interested in my career and MK murder case.'

'It's my responsibility, baby, to see you in very top.'

Then suddenly they were interrupted by a phone call from Aditya. His wife picked up his mobile which kept on the table in front of the TV in living room and handed over to him.

He took mobile from his wife and answered,' Hello dude, what's up?'

'Dude, I was interrogated by the police just now. I told him everything, he said that he will state as Akbar and I were not the suspects.'

'Good news, dude. Then why your voice so dull. Enjoy man.'

'Hey, you heard correctly what I said. He said that he will consider and state as Akbar and I were not the suspects. Understand!' Aditya raised his voice.

'What do you mean?'

'YOU ARE A MURDERER.'

'What! Are you joking?' Prasad exclaimed.

'You are a murderer, the police said that you are a murderer but he will confirm after the special team submits their report.'

'I am not a murderer. Hey! first tell me what you told to the police?'

'I told him everything.'

'Everything! What everything includes?'

'From my first introduction with you in our college to the last day of our college, a warning to MK at college and our toxic conversation in Durga Wines.'

Prasad was muted with his friend's innocence and ended the call. 'Now the police men were thinking that I am a murderer.' He said to his wife.

His wife brought him a glass of water, he sipped and relaxed on their giant couch.

After few minutes, the door was knocked as the door bell was not working. They both looked at each other and his wife slowly stood, moved from her place with some fear, shiverers in her body and opened the door while Prasad was still stuck on the couch.

'Hi, my name is Raghav, the police.' some voice came out at the door.

Prabha greeted him and said, 'Yes sir, Come in. Take a seat.' switched on the fan and moved to kitchen for bringing cool drink from the refrigerator.

Prasad also greeted him before the police entered into their home, 'Come in, sir, Sit comfortably. I had not expected you to be here. What's the update on MK murder case?'

'See, Mr. Prasad, I have some questions regarding this murder case. So, I have to clear from you today itself.' Police responded while sitting on couch.

Prabha kept two glasses of cool drinks on table and stood aside.

Prasad said, 'Yes sir, you can ask any question. I will always cooperate with you.'

'You are a Murderer.' Police said sipping cool drink.

'No, I am not a murderer. Listening Aditya's words, you are portraying me as a murderer. It's just a word spitted from an alcoholic man.'

'I understand that you said the toxic words but I am not considering that, where you were on the day of MK Murder.'

'My wife and I both were invited for lunch to his home by my friend Akbar. So, we both were stayed in his house since morning.'

'Where you were on the day of MK Murder? I don't ask you another question until you answer this question.'

'Sir, we both were in Akbar's home. You can ask Akbar and his parents.' His wife said in between.

The police man angered, pointed finger at her and said, 'Keep shut your mouth.'

Prasad said, 'Sir, please behave in a proper way with women.'

'Okay, sorry madam.'

The police added, 'You came to your home at that night around eight from beach road. You both left Akbar's home at evening four and dropped your wife at your home. Then reached beach road within an hour. You met Mohan Krishna there and warned him not to marry Fathima as you had some special desire towards her. You both fought each other and you took your pen from your pocket to kill him but it slipped from your hands. But as your preplanning, you kept the vegetable cutting knife on the sands of seashore. You took it and cut his throat with that sharp bladed vegetable cutting knife. Many people came there to help him and you escaped from there. This was the real story happened on that day.'

He continued, 'So, you are a murderer, our special team found your blue ball point pen on the crime spot and your plain brown colored hand kerchief you used for gripping the knife.'

'I am not a murderer. I will tell you everything what happened on that day.'

15

Prasad continued his version saying, what happened on the day of MK murder.

I remember the date: 20 March 2022 Sunday. I was about to reach Akbar's home. I had been very excited all morning as Prabha and I was invited to his home after a long time that too with my partner. After my marriage, this was the first time Prabha and I were going to someone's home for Biryani Party. During our first year of engineering, Akbar invited me to the party but after that, he became a miserable man, but still, he was my bestie.

Prabha and I were climbing the upstairs to Akbar's floor. It was about afternoon twelve thirty when I knocked on his door. His mom opened it and welcomed us in.

As I had often been there, she knew me well, but the first time I was with my beautiful wife. For me, Akbar's home never meant too many formalities. I was with my partner, so I had to act polite and mature. I was having some water when she told me that Akbar was not at home and his mobile was switched off.

'Wow! And he asked me not too late.' I murmured myself.

A little later, there was another knock on the door. As Akbar's mom was in the kitchen, I got up from my chair to open it. It wasn't Akbar, it was Akbar's dad.

'How are you, Prasad? How are you, Prabha?' Akbar's dad said politely with both of us at a time.

'How much polite was Akbar's dad, my dad was also there, he was never polite with me.' I thought myself comparing fathers.

'He's not on time all the time to home,' he irritated.

For the next half an hour, the three of us talked, while we both ate lunch made by Akbar's mother without Akbar. This might not sound decent, but nobody could predict his arrival. The biryani was very tasty and spicy.

After lunch, we moved to the giant sofa in the living room, sitting comfortably.

'How about publishing your first book?' Akbar's dad asked.

'Uncle, I was searching for a real story to launch the debut of my first novel.' I replied and said, 'I don't know how much time it takes to get it published.'

I dialed Akbar from my mobile, but his mobile was still switched off.

It was around evening four and still, we were waiting for Akbar.

A little later, there was another knock. Akbar's mom opened the door.

'What happened to your mobile? Why do you keep it switched off?' Akbar's mom shouted, opening a door.

'No Charging, mom,' Akbar sang loud.

I managed my anger toward him and acted very politely as I was around my wife and his parents. I observed his face and he was feeling some tense. I asked the reason for getting late and he said, simple sorry to both of us. I have never seen him before. He was worried about something.

'He was hiding something.' I thought to myself. I said bye to him but there was no response from him. We said bye to auntie and uncle, and left from there with some kind of unhappiness in our hearts. We left his home around evening four.

While driving to my home from Akbar's home, I have been received a phone call from an unknown number. I ignored that call as I was on driving. But still I was getting the repeated calls from the same number. So, I stopped my bike aside and answered the call.

'Hey dude, how are you? Have you forgotten me? It's Suresh, Suresh Kumar Sahoo.' he communicated in a phone.

'I am fine, man. What's happening? No calls, No Texts, you changed your contact. We were trying to reach you.'

'Cool man, I came to Visakhapatnam, waiting for you at beach road. Come alone, Let's meet here.'

'Alone! Why man.'

'I want to go quickly. If they come, they were not let me go back.'

'Ok man, I will be within an hour.'

I started excitedly to meet him after long time and reached my favorite spot, looking around for him. He was nowhere and phoned him but the mobile has been switched off. I sat on the green bench watching at seashore.

It's almost half an hour waiting for him and calling his mobile but it's still switched off. I washed my dirty face and took hand kerchief from my pocket. I rubbed my wet face with plain brown colored hand kerchief and sat again on the same bench. Some bald man asked me a pen as he was writing a love letter to propose his girlfriend. I was in some frustration and angered on my friend Suresh but I fake smiled and given my new blue point pen.

I walked few steps to lift the phone call receiving from Aditya but I don't want to tell him that I had been fooled by someone. I ignored his calls as if he knows I was at beach road, he will kill me to come his home as his home was near to beach road just fifteen minutes to reach there.

I looked back and I have not found that bald man. No matter about the bald man but he took my new blue point pen. I tried calling Suresh once again but his phone was still switched off. So, I moved from there and reached straight to my home that night around seven thirty.

On that night around eight, someone knocked our door. I got up from my giant sofa to open it as my wife was in the pantry cooking dinner. I pulled it open to shouts of, 'Oh.... Dude.... Come in!'

It was Akbar. 'Hi Babu,' he greeted me with a fake smile. Seeing his face, I realized that he was still not right. I smiled and welcomed him in. I thought to not ask the reason for behaving strangely this afternoon. I decided to make him happy tonight and we recalled our college days. My partner called for dinner and we all three together had dinner. I was still confused about what happened to him that afternoon and why now he came again. But still, I managed to laugh and he was also making some jokes. We were laughing again and again.

That night, we were both in my room having an amazing time. Talking about our past and present. About those minimum girls in our class. About my lecturers, my broken love, my friends, and my enemies. About our ragging and many other good bad things.

We talked about our jobs. We kept talking for hours that night. It was around night eleven, his sleeping time. He smiled and looked at me, I understand that it was his sleeping time and he had to leave now.

He left our place with a grand smile on his face by saying good night to both of us.

Prasad ended telling his story to the police, which happened on the day of MK Murder.

The police man was very silent and maybe something was going around in his mind. Prabha and Prasad were also keen-sighted his face expecting some response from him.

Finally, he opened his mouth and said, 'Ok, anyhow it's unbelievable. I had to inquiry once again to one more person now. I will find the culprit as soon as possible.'

The policemen left from there and his sudden visit somewhat relaxation to Prasad as he exhaled the entire happened story on that day. But his mind still weighing a lot of questions, why Suresh switched off his mobile on that day, how his blue point pen and brown hand kerchief found on crime spot, why Akbar came home late after inviting us.

Prasad and his wife had a dinner around night eight thirty, he drank a milk and they both slept on bed.

It was night around ten, Prasad heard a sweet voice of a beautiful girl, calling: Hello, Prasad, how are you? I came here only for you.

Prasad opened his eyes and he saw a beautiful and attractive blue-eyed women covered her face with soft white scarf wearing white dress, looks like an angel fallen from another planet.

Prasad opened his eyes and he saw a beautiful and attractive blue-eyed women covered her face with soft white scarf wearing white dress, looks like an angel fallen from another planet. He saw for his wife on the bed, she was not there on the bed. He searched around his bed then the beautiful women opened her scarf, it was his wife, Prabha. He was surprised with her beauty, she was calling him, moving her hands in air towards her. He followed her, she was moving and moving out, stood at their door, opened the door and moved out of the house. He was still following her and telling her to wait but she was turning back and moving again to front.

Prasad was shocked with her weird behavior. She went into the elevator, he also followed her into the elevator. He closed the gate of elevator. She pressed the ground floor button, elevator was started moving on and she moved forward towards him, kissed on his lips. They both chewed the lower lips and he licked her tongue into his mouth up to fifteen minutes. Then she bent down, pulled down his pants with inner wear and held his hard penis into her mouth, sucking in and out.

Prasad opened his tee and he was full nude, he removed her white top and hooked her white bra, seducing her breasts, kissed all over her cheeks. He lifted her white skirt up, she removed it and then he removed her white panties. He inserted his penis into her shaved vagina and increased his pace of movement. She moaned louder than normal and he observed the lift, it was not in ground floor, it was moving from ground to the last eleventh floor and vice versa. They both were naked and moaning were increasing more louder now. He removed his penis out and some fear started in his body, his legs and hands shivering. He observed his wife, she was standing naked in front of him, covering her full face with her hair.

Prasad was calling her, but she stood without any movement in her body. He moved towards her, removed her hair which covered her face. He was astonished to see her, it was not his wife, Prabha. It was Fathima.

He stepped back and asked her, 'What you were doing here?'

'Prasad, I came here only for you. I know you had a desire on me.'

'But I am married.'

'But I am still unmarried.'

Prasad observed her face, it was changing to red color. He was still watching her face with his jaw opening and his throat becomes very thirsty. He bent downwards to remove his clothes, he heard a sweet voice again, 'Prasad, why you were wearing your clothes, now you need sex. I came here only for you.'

He gulped his throat and looked up at her, her face totally changed like a zombie face with blue eyed eyes and he was standing nude in front of zombie.

He heard another voice from his behind, but it's now a male voice, held a hand on his shoulders, he turned back slowly and observed. He was shocked double now; it was Mohan Krishna.

Prasad started pressing the buttons in the elevator to move on from this hell but the press buttons not working. He observed Mohan Krishna slowly, then suddenly he was disappeared. He relaxed and started pressing buttons again. The elevator stopped but the elevator door was not opening.

He heard the moaning and groaning sounds louder, he turned back with fear. Mohan Krishna also changed into Zombie, he observed that MK inserted his penis from the back entry of another Zombie women.

'Prasad, come here, I came here only for you.' Zombie women calling him in double voice.

Prasad trying to open the door and turned back, only one women Zombie appeared in front of him. She turned back and he observed the mirror in front of him, some blood flown from his throat. He kept hands on his throat but the blood was not flowing from it.

The women zombie laughed at him; Prasad was watching her movement towards him. Another head coming from Fathima's body, he stepped back but can't step as it was the end of the space. It was the head of Mohan Krishna. The two headed human being standing in front of him.

Prasad stepping back even he knew that he can't escape from the elevator. He accidentally knocked the mirror heavily; it was broken and he saw the two people out of the elevator in long shot, calling him to jump, raising their hands. He observed them very carefully, they were Aditya and Akbar. He smiled, relaxed and jumped out from the elevator. He was fallen out from the elevator but he can't see his friends, he observed his wife on his bed. It was another Saturday nightmare, he thought and moved to washroom for pee.

17

Prasad returned from the washroom and picked up his mobile. It was morning around seven. Someone had entered into his room, he was shocked, it was his wife and turned back, observed on the bed. No one was there on the bed. He was confused and thought it might be his nightmare.

It was Sunday, full of tasty, spicy and pleasing, sensing of Hyderabad Dum Biriyani unclogged the nostrils of everyone in the family of Akbar. It's very special day to them as it was cooked by the great Akbar.

They were celebrating the Biriyani Party all together with the essence of spicy flavors. The police men said he had to inquiry once again one more person. Prasad thought it maybe Akbar as he came late home on the day of MK murder.

Prasad had some doubts now on Akbar. Is he murdered MK, no he might not be, so why he was upset on that day? He wants to call him but again he thought that it's not a right time as police were going there. They will confirm them as murderers.

While Akbar and his family celebrating, the police man entered into their party location with normal uniform holding gun. No one had observed him as everyone was busy in moving their asses with a joyful celebration. The police put his strong hand on Akbar's shoulder from his back side. Akbar was in full laughing mode and turned back dancing, paused after seeing the police men behind him.

The police man whispered, 'Hey buddy, you murdered one innocent and celebrating here with your family. You were great man.'

'What! Murder, no, I have not murdered anyone.'

'Come let's discuss somewhere where there was no noise or any disturbance.'

Akbar's dad interrupted by seeing their conversation, 'Hey Akbar beta, Who's this?

'Dad, he's, my friend.'

'Friend! He's looking elder than you.'

'Ha...Dad, I mean my friend's dad, he's my friend's dad.'

'Oh! Ok, where's your friend then?'

Akbar Paused and added, 'Dad, he left just now as he had some important work.'

'Sir, eat Biriyani and go. My son cooked very tasty and spicy.'

The police said, 'Okay, sure sir, I will eat Akbar's tasty Biriyani.'

'Akbar, take uncle to your room.'

Akbar responded, 'Okay dad.' They both moved to his room which located on the terrace.

'Your room looking good but you are bad.'

'Sir, I am not a murderer. I don't know why you were projecting me as a murderer.'

'I will ask you just one question. Tell me correctly otherwise I kick you on your bloody black ass.'

'Sir, I told you everything. Nothing was there to tell you.'

'Answer my question now. Where were you on the day of MK murder?'

'I invited my friend Prasad and his wife for lunch to my home as they were newly wedded.'

'You invited them but you were planned and arranged someone to kill him.'

Akbar explained showing the agreements:

'Sir, I borrowed cash from Ali Khan six months ago for my business purpose. I was unable to repay him, we argued each other and I slapped him unexpected. The argument increased between us and then Sameer bhai, one of the political activists solved the situation by making agreement between us. I can show you agreements and you can inquiry about this. My father doesn't know about my borrowing, so I request them not to tell him.'

The police observed the agreements shown by Akbar and his voice lowed.

They both had lunch, tasty and spicy Hyderabad Dum biriyani prepared by Akbar.

'You are not a murderer but good chef.' The police man smiled and appreciated him.

The policemen left his place but Akbar observed his face that he was trying to trap in this murder case. Akbar moved on and enjoyed the biriyani party with the family.

Prasad was dialing Akbar; he was not lifting his call as he was in party. He wants to know what happened today with the police in Akbar's house. He can't go to Akbar's home as it's not just a party, it's also a religion party.

The next day morning, while Prasad was travelling to the temple on his car with his wife, he received a call from Akbar.

'Hello, Prasad, the police arrived to my home yesterday morning.'

'I know buddy but I have not called you morning as you were spending your time with your family. I don't want to disturb you.'

'But I have seen ten missed calls from you.'

'Yeah, I don't want to call you but my anxiety not stopped me to know what happened with the police in your home.'

Akbar smiled and said, 'Nothing was happened, it's just a small inquiry.'

'Okay, Okay, we will meet today evening around six at Railway Park.'

'Okay buddy.'

Prasad ended his call and continued his journey.

They reached the Simhachalam temple and took blessings from the lord Narasimha Swamy. After darshan, they had lunch at nearby restaurant and moved to home around evening four.

Prasad met Akbar around evening six at Railway Park. They both discussed about the police Raghav, and again decided to meet him.

Prasad said, 'We will meet him tomorrow, not today.'

'Okay.'

On the next day, Akbar and Prasad entered into the police station sitting in the waiting hall.

The constable saw them and said, 'Wait, I will inform sir.'

The constable entered into the cabin of Raghav and returned back, 'Sir was calling you both,' pointed his finger towards them.

Both Akbar and Prasad went into his cabin, 'Good Morning, sir.'

The police Raghav also greeted them too and asked, 'May I know the purpose of visiting me?'

Akbar asked, 'Sir, Is there any other suspects? You were projecting only us.'

'Akbar! It's almost the end of solving this case.'

'You mean there were other suspects, or you were thinking a murderer is one of us.'

'You three were not murderers. There was other four suspects.'

Prasad exclaimed, 'Other four suspects!'

'Yes, Prasad.'

'Sir, who they were?'

The police stood from his chair and removed a file from his desk behind him, hand overed to Prasad.

Prasad read,

Case Study of Mohan Krishna Murder Case:

Suspects:

1. Fathima – MK's Fiancée
2. Keshav Raj
3. Sanjay Kumar

4. Muhammad Khali – Fathima's Father

Prasad exclaimed and asked, 'Fathima! Why and how?

The police informed that she was the main suspect.

'She was the main suspect, then you said before it was me.'

'Actually, you three were not suspects, I used you three just to know the connections between Fathima and you three.'

Akbar and Prasad were surprised, looking theirs faces at each other.

The Police continued and explained why Fathima was a main suspect.

Fathima:

Fathima was born in a poor family. She had a great desire to marry a rich man. She wants to live like a queen. She found MK was a rich man and loved him for money. As their religion was different, their families not agreed for their marriage. They both fought with their families and at last their parents were agreed to marry them. Fathima had planned to kill him before marriage and jump with his all-property documents. But MK not agreed to sign the documents before marriage. She might be a maximum chance to murder him.

They both were listening his story with a silent mode, and asked about other suspects.

Keshav Raj:

Keshav was a childhood friend of MK; he was born in middle class family. MK and Keshav were used to spend their maximum time at MK Royal Palace. He knew everything about MK includes all his assets, his girlfriends, sex, enemies, what not everything. MK's father don't like Keshav as he was unable to reach his financial status. He warned Keshav maximum times to leave his son. MK assets tripled before one week of his marriage. As Keshav knew this, he might have a chance to kill Mohan Krishna only for money.

Sanjay Kumar:

He had some crush and desire on Fathima. Sometimes he used to touch her with sexual intention and took some videos without knowing them. One day, MK found videos of his girlfriend Fathima on his mobile. His mobile was loaded with full gallery of Fathima's photographs and videos. Some photographs were edited nude which made MK angered. They both fight each other and Sanjay got injured by MK. He might have a chance to kill him for revenge.

Muhammad Khali – Fathima's Father:

He was a religious man. He wants to marry her daughter with his friend Akhtar's daughter. But one day his daughter came to him and declared that she will marry MK even no one agrees. Khali was silent on that day and the next day he sent some of his people to warn MK. If he still not listens, told them to kill him. The war of love happened two years and finally he agreed for marriage but somewhere his heart and soul not accepting other religious man into his family. There was a chance to kill him as they warned MK many times.

The police Raghav informed them that still some inquiries were going on.

Akbar said, 'So, you used our three as snakes in your game.'

'Because of you three, I got some more suspects. I knew how this murder case was important to me as well as to Prasad. I want to help him to fulfill his dream. I hope this MK Murder case will be solved as soon as possible. This was a big challenge to both of us.'

Prasad and Akbar were silent, looking confused but somewhat happy that they were not suspects and Prasad will be an author soon.

While leaving the police station, Raghav said them to meet again tomorrow. They both left the police station with some happiness in their face. Prasad fake smiled and he was still in dilemma thinking about his blue ball point pen and his brown hand kerchief. He was also thinking about Fathima, how she can be the main suspect, how she can murder his lover and fiancée.

While moving to the parking area, Akbar observed Prasad's face and asked, 'What happened?'

'Nothing, worrying about my nightmares.' Prasad lied.

'Nothing to worry my friend, wait for two months. You will get a solution, or else we will meet another psychiatrist.'

'It's okay, I will wait for Mr. Chowdhury.'

They both moved to their homes around night seven, with great excitements over their faces.

19

It was a hot day with a hot news around the cool city. The people everywhere around the city discussing and chatting about her. That day was a relaxation to the three friends as they were like some happy prisoners releasing from a jail on the Independence Day for their good work. They were released from the MK Murder case. The policemen found a culprit and arrested but Prasad's heart still not believes that she was a murderer. He doesn't know what's the truth behind this murder but he had some hope that she will be not a murderer. *Is this the reason Raghav said to meet today?* He thought to himself.

That morning around ten thirty, Prasad met the police as Raghav said to meet him, Akbar had some work, so he doesn't come. Prasad wants to know how the police found culprit and arrested, for the purpose of his debut novel.

Prasad waited for two hours for Raghav in the waiting hall but he was not frustrated and angered as some excitement in his cherish face as he almost at the end of the story to become a published author soon.

His brain weighed many questions and he had to get some answers from the policemen, how his pen and handkerchief placed in a crime spot, who was the bald person, why she murdered MK. While all these questions cooking in his mind, the policemen entered into his cabin. He stood from the vintage brown bench which was placed opposite to the door of his cabin.

Everyone stood and respected him, some constables were decorated him with beautiful blossomed garlands on his neck as he arrested the murderer and solved the case. Some constables murmured that it was the first murder case which was delayed by him. Prasad heard some nearby prisoners were gossiping that the policemen will arrest someone to close the murder case as soon as possible.

The policemen, Raghav invited Prasad inside his cabin and he moved in with great excitement, greeted him and congratulated him for solving this murder case, also thanked him for giving them freedom from this murder case.

Raghav smiled and said,' You three were good at helping me to investigate and solve this murder case. Congratulations as you were the upcoming bestselling author.'

'Thank you, sir, for your appreciation. Hope my first debut novel will be a successful.'

Prasad asked him a full story about finding a culprit, taking his notebook and new blue pen from his blue string bag.

The police Raghav took a cigar from his pocket, lit a fire with his lighter and said, 'Sorry, sometimes, I will cigar due to over pressure from my department. I had some doubt on Fathima when the file of murder case hand overed to me by my superior but I thought to myself that she was loved more than ever by MK. So, I never involved her in this case.'

He released some smoke from the cigar and continued the story.

Fathima was born in a poor family to Muhammed Khali and Sheik Zoya. Since her childhood, she was fond of rich items such as jewelry, cars, Palaces and more. She was poor but her desires and dreams were rich. She had a crush on his classmate Imran as he was son of rich man in school days. After some years, she made a decision to marry only a rich man. She wants to live like a queen. In college days, she found MK was a rich man and loved him only for money. She knew that all properties and assets were in the name of MK. She forced MK to marry and transfer all his assets in her name.

As their religion was different, their families not agreed for their marriage. She thought that her plan was failed and but she had an alternative plan. They both were struggled and fought with their families and finally their parents were agreed to marry them. But Fathima's main intention was not a marriage, she needs only his money not MK. Fathima had planned to murder him before marriage and went off with his all-signed property documents. But MK not agreed to sign the documents before marriage.

One day morning, she met her one of the school friend Ameer and explained everything to him. They both were dealt that she will give forty percentage of his all assets after the task was finished.

She sketched the entire murder plan before one month of his murder. As per her plan, she needs a person to made him as a murderer. She knew that you loved her very much in college, so she decided to make you as the main suspect of this murder case. She received your contact number from the Facebook profile you mentioned. She also knew whereabouts of you and your friends. She found that you were not in contact with Suresh. She arranged Ganesh, a bald person as Suresh where you communicated with him on phone that the day of murder.

Ameer bought a new and very sharp-edged vegetable cutting knife from the nearby local market. Ganesh bought a new Airtel Sim and inserted in his basic mobile.

Her main plan was to bring MK to the room no. 201 where she booked in 'Chandra Lodge' at R.K Beach Road. After murdering him, she wants to take his fingerprints to sign on the property documents as per her plan.

On that day, she called MK in phone to meet R.K Beach Road. At first, he hesitated as he was busy in marriage planning works but she said that it was very important to meet.

It was around afternoon three, he arrived there and met her. She hugged him tightly and held his hands closely. They walked around the seashore and chit chatted a romantic talk. After few minutes, she slowly informed that she booked a room in nearby lodge. But he was confused and hesitated, his romantic desire was uncontrollable. He agreed with her decision and moved forward but he don't know her plan as he trusted her. She was an angel to him but he was unable to find a demon inside her.

Before their entry into the room, the two men Ganesh and Ameer were already in the room which was locked outside by Fathima and kept the keys with the reception of the lodge. Fathima and MK moved into the lodge, she took the room keys and moved the upstairs as the lift was not working.

Ganesh stood behind the curtains of the dark room holding the sharp-edged knife, worn the white colored hand gloves and Ameer hid under the bed, he also worn the white colored hand gloves. They covered their faces with a mask similar to the face masks worn in the popular web series 'Money Heist'.

They both walked at the door and she took the room keys from her maroon-colored stylish hand bag and kept a key in a hole of locked door and moved it. She opened the door and reached to the switch board on the left side wall of the room. She had switched on the lights and a fan. They both walked together and slept on a bed, holding hands together. He gazed her eyes and allowed his lips to smooch her pink lips. She pushed him back and said to wait some minutes as she will go to wash room and return. She went in to washroom and he sat on the bed.

Ameer slowly moved from under the bed and came behind MK. He closed his mouth very hardly with his gloved hands from behind. MK was moaned heavily and unable to breathe himself. Ganesh moved in front of MK and took a hidden knife slowly from his backside of his worn shirt. He cut MK's throat with the sharp knife and the blood flown from his throat like a water from the tap. Fathima came from the washroom with a bucket of water and MK fallen his tears from his eyes as he understood that she was a master behind his murder.

They cut the right-hand thumb for thumb stamp for signing the documents. Fathima cleaned the blood stains on the floor and the few stains flown around the bed. They tied with a piece of cloth at MK throat to control the blood leakage. Within few minutes, MK died. They removed the pumpkins from the sack which they brought before entering into the lodge and they kept the dead body in that same sack which was bought by Ganesh from the local market.

Then Ganesh called you from new Airtel sim which he inserted in his basic mobile and communicated as your friend Suresh. Their plan succeeds to bring you at crime spot. He waited at the green bench by switching off the mobile after visiting your entry towards that same bench. As Fathima told him to ask you pen as she knew you were a writer helped maximum people in writing love letters in college and can't move anywhere without pen. So, he asked you a pen and you received a call from someone. You stepped to talk on a phone and then he hid between the crowd. You removed a hand kerchief from your pocket and rubbed your face but you not kept it in your pocket as you were in hurry and also worried about Akbar's behavior was confused on that day.

After observing your movement from there, Ganesh removed hand gloves from his pocket and worn it, took your handkerchief with handed gloves. He kept both your pen and handkerchief in a plastic cover and moved to a lodge again.

Ameer and Fathima were waiting and tensed about the task sitting at the sack of dead body. Then Ganesh entered with a great smile like a winner of the lottery ticket. They both understood that they accomplished a task successfully.

They waited sometime and thought that they have to throw the dead body as soon as possible at the beach road.

It was around evening four thirty, they moved with a sack of dead body by stairs as the lift was not working. The receptionist observed them and he thought that they were moving pumpkins as he saw they moved pumpkins before entering into lodge. He asked that he can help them if possible but they smiled and denied his help.

Ameer moved to car parking and up lifted the dead body at the backside of car. It was just ten minutes to reach the spot they planned and moved at the beach road. Ganesh and Ameer slowly dropped the sack of the dead body from their car and moved it to the sandy seashore. Ganesh removed your pen and handkerchief from a plastic bag and thrown near the dead body. Ameer slowly sat on the sand and kept the knife on the seashore. The public thought that some seller was selling something to Fathima as she moved first from there and Ameer next to her. Then Ganesh moved into heavy crowd and left from there.

They planned everything but they were unable to get the original documents of properties. They tried three to four times and theft the documents from MK house but they were not the original documents. Their plan was failed in getting the documents of assets signed but they succeeded in killing MK.

Our clue team officially found the sharp knife, your blue pen and your handkerchief. We caught Ganesh three days ago and inquired, he spoke out all the truth behind this MK murder. We arrested her and these two men who partially accomplished the bad task.

The policeman ended the crime story and revealed everything while Prasad took notes with his new blue ball point pen for his crime thriller debut novel.

Prasad was excited as he got a story, came out of the police station around afternoon two, saying thanks to the police, stood at the parking area and dialed his wife.

Her mobile was ringing but she was not lifting her call. Prasad tried three to four times, but still she was not lifting a call.

Prasad received a message notification on his mobile screen, it's from an unknown number, he read: *You will be the reason of her death.*

Prasad tensely dialed her wife again and again, but still she was not lifting his call.

20

Prasad dialed her wife again and again, but still she was not lifting his call. He drove back to his home, knocked the door but not opened. He dialed her again, he can hear the ringing tune of her mobile but she was not lifting. He knocked the door again and again, but still not opened.

Some hand touched his shoulder from his behind, it's his wife, Prabha. Prasad relaxed and asked her, 'Where have you gone? I am calling you since an hour.

'Relax baby, I went to fishery market for buying your favorite fish. I forgot my mobile in our room itself.'

Prasad muted without creating any scene and entered into the home, sitting on the giant couch, thinking about the message he received from an unknown. He ignored the message and smiled at his wife without telling her about it.

On the next day, Thursday morning around ten, Prasad enquired Akbar about arrival of Psychiatrist from U.S.A. Akbar responded,' No, he will come in the month of June only.'

Prasad was still looking happy and took his laptop, started writing his first draft titled the Novel *'He was Murdered'* and kept the target to release his first book in the month of June.

The days were changing, but his nightmares on Saturdays were not changed, he completed his first draft within a month. He was still receiving a message from different unknown numbers but he decided to ignore all the messages until his completion of first book. MK murder case was still in a court, Fathima was still in jail, her lawyers were fighting for the case.

Two months gone, it's a hot month of June, Prasad was waiting for this month to meet his friend's Psychiatrist uncle and also for his first book launch.

Prasad was trouble in packing his heavy luggage, his wife helped and arranged his clothes in proper way in his favorite-colored sky blue American Tourister trolly. Finally, she successfully packed his luggage with low burden. They both were excited as his debut novel was ready to launch. So, they were planned first a small devotional tour to Tirupati and after a week, a romantic tour to Ooty, but the destiny planned in other way as he had received a call from the publications team that they planned to launch his first book tomorrow on 22 June 2022 on two schedules, one at Visakhapatnam Beach Road morning and other book launch at Diveagar Beach, Raigad district of Maharashtra on the same day night. His debut novel titled **'He Was Murdered'**, launching tomorrow.

His package of luggage was not cancelled but his trips to devotional and romantic destinations were postponed. But he was not felt bad as it was his dream of being author. It's his first best astonishing and cherish moment in his life. He had informed to the launch event organizer and the publications team about the guests. He invited the policeman, Mr. Raghav as a special guest to book launch and He also planned to invite his favorite Telugu actor 'Victory Venkatesh or Daggubati Venkatesh' through his personal assistant but due to his busy movie schedule, he denied his invitation.

On the next day, it was morning around ten, Prasad booked ola cab from his home to the beach road for him and his wife. They will reach the location within thirty minutes. His friends Aditya and Akbar reached there already decorating the stage with the launch event organizer and with the publications team. The police men Raghav about to reach within forty minutes. The Book launch event will start around morning eleven.

They reached beach road within thirty minutes and they had been provided A.C room to relax until the launch starts. They both sat on the chairs provided in the room. He got some tensed and nervous with some great excitement. His wife observed his nervousness and he was controlling with a fake smile on his face. It's his first book launch event. And he had some shyness and stage fear. She touched his hands with a great smile on her face, encouraged him saying, 'It will be a big successful book launch event. Be confident, Be strong with no fear. You can do it.' Her words build his confidence but he had another diversion in his mind saying that Fathima was an innocent. His image reflection says that She was a murderer. He was confused but he thought whatever It is, now, he is an author.

He had been observed the stage which was decorated with beautiful fragrant roses and various blossoms of flowers on the magnificent seashore, aside the sounds of waves encouraging him very pleasant to launch the book quickly as soon as possible. He had not expected the heavy crowd for his book launch event, they may be the visitors around the beach, no matter who they were but he had the visitors to his first book launch. Some were gossiping that some celebrities naming themselves as Salman Khan, Pawan Kalyan, Chiranjeevi and different names from various film industries, even Prasad don't know some of the names, will be launching. Whatever the Gossips were, but he enjoyed it very much. Some people on the seashore whistling and making noise to start the launch soon.

The beautiful female anchor walked on the stage with a stunning smile on her face, adjusting her tomato red colored saree and brushing her fallen hair on her round blue eyes with her fingers. The youth in the crowd whistling by seeing her. She welcomed every one of the publications team on the stage, then she invited the policemen to come on the stage but still police Raghav were not arrived. She called of the next name as Mr. and Mrs. Prasad Babu Galla. Then they both walked on the stage with great smile on their faces. Then after she invited the Local M.L.A and some politicians. Everyone took their seats and one of the seats for the police beside Prasad was still vacant.

The beautiful anchor started praising Prasad as he was only the author in this world. He doesn't know how his story will be popular but the script of this anchor will be definitely a grand successful. Then the police appeared like a sudden storm on the stage with a smile on his face, greeting politicians first and sat beside Prasad, greeted him with a fake smile and congratulated. He too greeted and thanked for helping him to get a content.

The anchor invited the M.L.A Shashidhar Reddy to speak some lines about Prasad. *'What he knows about me,'* Prasad thought to himself.

M.L.A took some written paper from his personal assistant; it may be a written script. He started his speech about Prasad:

The debut author Mr. Prasad Babu Galla, had written the real crime story very well about the recent MK murder case solved by the sincere police officer Mr. G. Raghav Sai. I appreciate the author for his guts to make a script and publish the true story. He knew that he gets fake calls and warnings from the people of murderer. But still he didn't fear of anyone, he followed his passion.

He was born in the middle-class family to Mr. and Mrs. Demudu. His parents were very lucky to have a gut author who believes himself and follows his passion. Everyone must follow your passion and achieve a success like him. We don't have much time otherwise one hour was not enough to talk about him. I was ending this speech now.

Thank You,

Jai Hind.

It was an awkward silence, no response from the audience. Prasad was eagerly waiting for claps and whistles from the audience. Then suddenly, he heard a clap of a child from the third line of the row and everyone started clapping and whistling. He was very happy and waited long time for this cherish moment. His darling kept a handkerchief in his hand to wipe his fallen tears, He don't know when his tears felt down from his black eyes. He happily took handkerchief and wiped his tears and controlled his over excited happiness.

The beautiful anchor again adjusted her saree showing her slim waist to the audience and invited some other politicians. One by one approached to mic stand and appreciated Prasad. Then the police man was invited to speak some words about him.

He moved to the mic stand and started his speech.

I have seen the writing skills of the debut author Mr. Prasad Babu Galla. I observed the burning desire of his passion when the first time I inquired him of the murder case. He came to me for the story script to collect from me. I helped him in producing the true crime story of MK murder case. I was surprised as the both murderer and the guy who was murdered, was his classmates in college, but still he helped me to investigate. I really appreciate the author for his guts to make a script and publish the true story. We both travelled together in solving the mystery of this murder case. It was an astonishing journey between us. I also appreciate his friends Aditya and Akbar who helped me to investigate.

Thank you for giving me an opportunity to speak about the passionate debut author.

He ended his speech aloud with a great excitement and exhausted his happiness with a chuckle on his face.

Finally, Prasad was invited to take his words about the book launch and started his version of speech.

I thank everyone who decorated the stage very astonishingly by their name one by one. I thank the audience who stood in front of me, I hope, I attract you by reaching you through my books. I had to thank the police Mr. Raghav as he helped me a lot in getting the content. I thank my friends who stood behind me to reach this stage. I thank especially my beautiful life partner who motivated all the time and encouraged to write this crime story. I paused my speech of happiness and wiped some shining drops from my eyes falling on my cheeks. And continued to invite the book launch by M.L.A.

Prasad ended his speech and stood at his seat beside the police. M.L.A moved to the middle of the stage and pulled the curtain where the banner of his book cover located at. It was designed marvelous, unique and attractable by Prasad itself.

His debut novel launched successfully completed and dined at Novotel with his life partner, friends, the police and the politicians.

While moving from the location, Prasad received a text message from an unknown number.

'*Your arrival of Success is from the departure of her failure.*'

Prasad replied, 'Who are you?'

'*It's better not to know me but Your ignorance of my messages kills the people around you.*'

While Prasad reading text message, her wife observed his tension and asked,' What happened? You look tensed.'

'Nothing,' he fakes smiled at her and moved to their home.

21

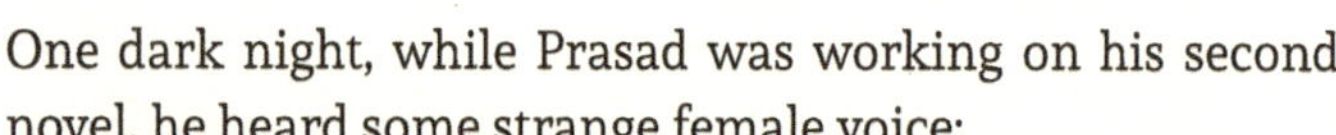

One dark night, while Prasad was working on his second novel, he heard some strange female voice:

'Your first book was incomplete; it had all fake story.'

He searched for a voice within his room, his wife was sleeping on the bed. It's not her voice.

He heard the sound of knocking door, he shut down his laptop and moved from his room, walked baby steps towards the door. The sound increased, increased heavily and louder and louder continuously increasing.

Prasad shouted,' Hey Can't you wait? I am opening the door.'

The sound stopped immediately, he opened the door slowly, looked out but no one was there. He closed the door and moved back. Again, the door was knocked by someone, he opened again, no one was there. He closed the door again and turned back, he saw a beautiful woman, it's his wife.

His wife asked, 'What happened? What were you doing here?'

'Someone knocked our door, I opened but no one was there.'

'I have not heard any knocked sound.'

'I heard some female voice: Your first book was incomplete; it had all fake story.'

'That's me, I told you this when I was asleep.'

'But when I saw you, you were slept.'

'I haven't got any response from you. So, I slept without disturbing you.'

'So why you said like that?'

'It looks like an incomplete fake story for me.'

Prasad muted his conversation and thought himself,' It was Saturday night around twelve, Still I didn't get any nightmare. But who knocked the door, Is it part of the nightmare? Then my conversation with my wife is not real.'

His wife interrupted and said,' Baby, Are you alright?'

'Yes, I am alright.' He smiled at her and confirmed that it's real.

Prasad hugged her tightly in his arms and kissed on her cheeks, laughed loudly, lifted her and dropped her on the bed.

She confused and smiled with him saying good night, slept on the bed closing brown rug over her body.

He took his mobile and texted Akbar,' I didn't get any nightmare.'

Prasad switched off the lights and the first time he slept peacefully on Saturdays in his entire life.

On the next day, Akbar dialed him and communicated, 'Is it real or just joking on your nightmare?'

'Yes, it's real buddy. I can't believe how it happened.'

'Anyhow, congrats and Psychiatrist uncle called me that he arrived today morning.'

'I think now no need of his favor as everything was alright.'

'You have to wait for next Saturday, if you don't get any nightmare, then you don't need of his favor.'

'But I had another problem now.'

'What's that?'

'We will meet tomorrow.'

'Okay.'

'Bye, bye.'

They both ended the call, Prasad looked his mobile screen, he received a text message.

He opened and read:

'Know the real within her; Know the real within him.'

He replied *'Who is her? Who is him?'*

There was no response from the stranger. Prasad waiting for a reply, looking at his mobile screen. But still no response.

Prasad thought to himself,' *Why strange things happen to me? Strange Murder case, Strange Nightmare and now Strange Messages.'*

On the next day morning, Prasad looked at his author sales dashboard, his debut novel sales were increasing day by day more than the previous month. He was very excited and shared this good news with his beautiful goddess. But she was so dull and her face was not shiny as before.

He has been asked the reason of her dull face, she said that she heard that Fathima suicided and hospitalized. She has been in critical situation. She may not survive; his wife paused and cried the first time in her life.

Prasad said, 'Karma will be back; she killed his own boyfriend. She may feel guilty now. The destiny welcomed her to kill herself.'

'Karma is for everyone; don't know what's the truth, don't know what's the lie, don't know what is good, don't know what is bad.'

Prasad muted with her words and thought to himself,' Is the story I heard from one side is the false, and other side is true?'

His wife encouraged and motivated him to get the story from the police but she had not told him to believe the police.

If Prasad made a mistake, he had to solve this but some guilty weighs within his heart. If he was right then he never surrenders to anyone.

Her words about Karma discouraged his morning mood and strength. He wants to know whether the police Raghav cased a fille against Fathima was True or False.

After his mind distraction, he drove his new red colored car Maruti Ertiga to the beach road for a peace of mind. He sat alone on the rocks at an ocean, the waves insulting him for his success which arrived by making someone accused falsely. He can't feel happy as somewhat weighing in his heart with guiltiness.

Many questions rising in his mind: *Is Fathima not a murderer? Is the policemen Raghav fooled me by telling a fake story? Then who murdered MK? How to find the answers to my questions? Am I sinner? Am I selfish?*

The notification sounds on his mobile screen interrupted his questions, he took his mobile from his pocket and read one of the notifications: *You received one message.* He opened the message and read:

'*Stay tuned, Your Karma will be back.*'

Prasad replied: '*Who are you? Why you were texting me messages?*'

He didn't get any response and then he dialed to that number but it's an automated call: *You were calling the number is currently switched off, please try later.*

Prasad thought himself, 'Who's this? Why I was hearing the word Karma today?'

He dialed Akbar but he didn't lift his call and then he moved to the same green bench where he lost his blue pen and handkerchief. He remembered the past what happened on that day and the bald man, who took a pen from him.

Someone interrupted his thoughts, what happened to him, yes, he was, he has seen the bald man now on flash, wearing a blue colored full hand sleeves shirt, plain black colored pant. He searched around him; the bald man was moving quickly. Prasad followed him but the bald man ran faster and faster, he missed him.

Then to whom the policemen caught and arrested on that day. Prasad called the police Raghav but his call was busy.

Prasad received a message from unknown again: *You made a mistake, big mistake. Your Karma will be back.*

'Who's this?'

'*I am your friend till now, but you are my enemy now.*'

'*What I did to you? We will meet and talk together.*'

'*You knew what you did, the destiny will bring us together soon. But Karma not leaves you.*'

Prasad thought to himself, 'He or she was my friend till now, but now my enemy. Who's this?'

He moved and reached at his car. Something was written on his car window glasses with red paint: '*Go and meet her.*'

'Her means Who, Fathima!' Prasad thought to himself and received a message again: *She was admitted in King George Hospital.*

He has been confirmed that this unknown stranger talking about Fathima, but how's this man/woman linked with her.

Prasad texted him: *What you were to her?*

'*I am also her friend like you.*'

Then he or she might be a common friend to us in our college. Prasad thought to himself.

Prasad received message again: *You have a beautiful car and a beautiful wife. They can destroy your life or else someone may destroy their life. It may be your Karma.*

What's the meaning of this message? Prasad thought to himself, *what he or she was telling about my car and my wife. My car will destroy my life – that means accident. My wife will destroy my life – that means she will kill me. Why she will kill me, or else someone destroy their life. Who and why kills my wife, who and why ruins my car?*

Prasad drove his car fast to reach home, calling his beautiful wife on phone but her mobile was switched off. Tried and tried, still her mobile was switched off.

22

Prasad reached his home within a few minutes and knocked on the door but his wife does not open the door. He called by her name and then she opened the door slowly.

She cried aloud and hugged him tensely with fear on her face and shivering body.

Prasad relaxed her and said by giving her a glass of water, 'Cool baby, relax! What happened?'

'Some woman in a black suit covering her face with a black mask holding a small hammer in one hand appeared in our living room, destroyed my mobile with a hammer and made it into small pieces.'

'Are you sure, Is she a woman?'

'Yes, she is a woman. She said to give you a small piece of paper written on it: *Go and meet her.*'

'How she came into the home which the door was closed inside?'

'I don't know.'

Prasad watched every corner of the room in his flat, he observed that the window was broken in the washroom and some footsteps landed on the ground and followed into their living room.

'She arrived through the washroom by breaking the window through the hammer and entered into the living room, destroyed the mobile with the same hammer, and went out

through the main door after warning my wife.' Prasad thought to himself, after seeing the broken pieces of the mobile.

'Can we give a complaint to the police?'

'No, first we have to meet Fathima.'

'But how Fathima related to this lady stranger?'

'It will be known only after meeting Fathima.'

Prasad received a call from his friend Akbar, he muted sometimes and lifted his call.

'Hello, Akbar. What's up?'

'Hello, Dude. Do you know that Aditya was missing for the past week?'

'What!'

'Yes, dude. His parents have complained to the police station. I thought he went to the camp with his fiancée Ashrita.'

'I too thought the same.'

'I want to meet you right now.'

'We can meet at King George Hospital.'

'Hospital! What happened? Is anything serious?'

'Come there, I want to talk with you.'

'Okay, bye, bye.'

Prasad ended the call and said to his wife,' Be here, I will return as soon as possible.'

'Baby, don't leave me. She may come again.'

'No, she will not come until I complete the task.'

'Task?'

'Yes, Task. The task is given by the lady stranger to go and meet Fathima. If any problem, call me on our landline phone.'

'Okay baby.'

Prasad received a notification from an unknown contact on his mobile screen:

HE WAS MURDERED

'*Come fast, waiting for you at the hospital.*'
(TO BE CONTINUED..........)

Epilogue

July 2022

King George Hospital, Visakhapatna

Prasad made a very big mistake, his heartAll throbbing to massive pain the first time. He stepped into the King George Hospital ICU and he was overrun with guilty emotions. After a few minutes, he was standing outside the ICU door; Fathima was behind a green curtain.

'You are the reason behind her deteriorating condition, how can you publish the book without inferring the real,' her father cried at him with some displeasure incur.

Prasad felt blameworthy about his words and he stood immoral before Fathima's father. All relatives around the waiting hall stared at him with anger.

He met the doctor and enquired about her recovery.

'Rare Chance; Her condition is getting worse. She poisoned heavily and passed through the blood. She was unable to breathe. We are planning to put her on a ventilator but her family can't afford the cost.' the doctor said in a concerned tone.

'Can I visit her now?'

'Yes, you can but don't make her talk.'

Prasad went inside ICU behind the green curtain with a heavy heart. He went near her. There was blood around her lips. She lay with her mouth open and her eyes closed. He has seen this type of horrible moment in his life when his mother demised, now again with Fathima. He wished he could have given his birth if God provided a life exchange opportunity but he was helpless. He came out of ICU with great difficulty.

His wife just came and stood outside the ICU and hugged her crying first time saying, 'I am sinful, and her life was at risk because of me.'

She whispered something which gave him strength and he took a bench outside ICU.

Prasad understood what she whispered in his ears but he was still hopeless and sinful. She whispers to afford the bill for the hospital including the ventilator cost. She forced him to rewrite the book again with a great apology for knowing the real. He wishes he could rewind and save Fathima.

His wife said, 'You are not a sinner, you are Hero. Let's find who is a sinner and help Fathima.'